Beguiling the Earl

Suzanna Medeiros

Copyright © 2014 Saozinha Medeiros

All rights reserved.

ISBN-13: 9780991823772

This is a work of fiction. Names, characters, places, and incidents are the product of the author's imagination or are used fictitiously. Any resemblance to actual events, locales, or persons, living or dead, is purely coincidental.

OTHER BOOKS BY SUZANNA

Dear Stranger

Landing a Lord series
Dancing with the Duke
Loving the Marquess
Beguiling the Earl
The Unaffected Earl—coming soon

Hathaway Heirs series
Lady Hathaway's Indecent Proposal
Lord Hathaway's New Bride—coming soon

DEDICATION

To Maria and Aida for being the best sisters I could
have asked for.

CONTENTS

ACKNOWLEDGMENTS

Thank you to everyone who offered support and input during the writing of this book. In particular, Aida Amaral, Maddy Barone, Maria Medeiros, and Maaike van der Leeden.

I also want to thank my editor, Anne Victory, for being so good at what she does!

CHAPTER ONE

1807

CATHERINE EVANS SHOULDN'T have been bored. She was in London at a crowded ball and was dancing with a handsome man. Heaven knew she'd been anticipating her first season for months—ever since she'd learned the previous fall that her sister would soon be marrying the Marquess of Overlea. That event had completely changed their lives for the better. Until the day her sister had made the announcement, she'd never thought she would actually find herself in town, attending all manner of balls and other evening entertainments. She'd been looking forward to spring with increasing excitement ever since.

Now, less than one month into the season, she was already tired of the endless social demands. Balls at least once a week, musicales, routs, and visits to the theater. She'd imagined the whole experience would be more exciting. Knew it would have been if one man were present, a man who'd promised to be here to dance with her when she'd met him last fall.

She smiled politely at her partner, Viscount Thornton, as their gloved hands met briefly while they moved through the figures of the country dance. He was only a few years older than her, and she had to admit he was very handsome with his blond hair and blue eyes. She couldn't help but measure him against the man she still looked for at every ball, and in comparison he seemed little more than an eager boy.

When the dance was over, he led her back to her sister. She accepted his compliments on her grace of movement with cool reserve and redirected the conversation back to the much safer subject of the weather. Thornton made no secret of his admiration for her, and she suspected he would become a nuisance if she encouraged him even slightly.

It was with some relief that she spotted Louisa and Nicholas a few feet away. He stood with his broad back to the dance floor, and it was only as she neared him that she remembered her brother-in-law had worn a coat of deep blue while this man wore black. A fluttering sensation started low in her belly.

When Louisa spotted her, she said something to her companion and he turned to greet her. The fluttering sensation blossomed into a full riot of butterflies, and she was powerless to stop the smile that spread across her face.

"Kerrick," she exclaimed.

She managed a quick smile of dismissal in Thornton's direction before hurrying across the last few feet that separated her from the man she'd been waiting to see again. She stopped just short, her breath far too uneven to have been caused by the light exercise of the dance. She almost reached for his hands but resisted the impulse. She'd learned enough during her time in London to know such a display of affection would cause raised eyebrows and not a small amount of gossip.

"Miss Evans. It is so nice to see you again."

He smiled down at her, his blue eyes crinkling at the corners, and joy unfurled within her. He was just as handsome as she remembered.

"You devil, you promised to dance with me during my season. And here we are, a full three weeks in, and you haven't attended even one of the balls."

He affected an expression of exaggerated dismay.

"You wound me to accuse me of such negligence. Unfortunately, I had pressing matters to attend to which kept me from town."

She pretended to give his words careful consideration before replying. "I'll forgive you. But just this once."

His eyes shone with amusement. "Wretch."

She could only beam in reply. He turned back to Louisa, and Catherine had to be careful not to let her disappointment show.

"Have you received word from your brother?"

After learning the previous fall that Louisa had accepted the marriage proposal of Nicholas Manning, the Marquess of Overlea, their brother John had been furious. Nicholas's uncle had ruined their father and John couldn't bring himself to believe Louisa would align herself with that family. Louisa had hoped their brother would come around to accepting the marriage in time, but instead John had run off, leaving behind a note that stated he'd enlisted the help of a family friend in purchasing a commission in the army.

"No," Louisa said. "I've written to him but have heard nothing after his first reply." Her voice faltered before she continued. "I am so worried about him. He was never one to be so reckless."

Annoyance swept through Catherine when Kerrick

took hold of her sister's hand and gave it a quick, reassuring squeeze. "Most young men are rash, but fortunately we eventually outgrow it. I am sure John is well."

Before Catherine could remind the pair that she was still present, they were interrupted by an older couple approaching their small group. The man was of average height and build, his thinning hair liberally sprinkled with gray. His wife, however, was a striking woman whose dark hair was only starting to show signs of gray around the temples. Kerrick introduced them as Lord and Lady Worthington.

"We wondered when you would return to town," Lord Worthington said, turning his attention to Kerrick. "Rose has been quite put out by your negligence."

Kerrick lifted a brow and replied with cool equanimity. "One wouldn't surmise that from her behavior."

Catherine followed his gaze and spotted a young woman who had been announced earlier as Miss Rose Hardwick, daughter of Lord and Lady Worthington. The girl was about her own age and stood several feet away, surrounded by a group of young men who vied for her attention. Catherine wasn't surprised given the girl's almost radiant beauty. Rich chestnut curls framed a fair face that was uncommonly pretty. Her eyes sparkled, her lips pouted, and her cheeks bloomed with a rosy glow. With her pale hair and coloring, Catherine felt dull and lifeless by comparison.

Worthington shrugged. "She's young. Did you expect her to just stand in a corner and pine away for you?"

Lady Worthington was quick to add, "She merely flirts with those boys. She knows with whom her future rests."

Shock rolled through Catherine at the older woman's words, and her gaze swung back to Kerrick. His expression hadn't changed, but he didn't deny Lady Worthington's assertion.

"She seems to be enjoying herself quite well without my attention."

"Nonsense," Worthington said. "That's because she doesn't know you're here. We only just spotted you ourselves. Though I can't imagine why you wouldn't have sent word to us before now."

"I only just arrived last night," he said.

Worthington nodded, but it was clear Kerrick's reply hadn't satisfied him. He turned back to Catherine and Louisa. "Lady Overlea, Miss Evans, if you will excuse us?"

Catherine merely nodded in reply. She looked again

at Rose Hardwick, her thoughts full of the implication of the older man's words. She refused to believe there was an understanding between Rose and Kerrick. The fates wouldn't be so cruel.

Determined to learn the truth, she turned to question him, but Kerrick had already stepped away to speak to the older couple in private. Her dismay grew when they turned, as one, to approach Lord and Lady Worthington's daughter. The group of men dispersed at her father's presence, but a few hovered close by in case they were given another opportunity with her.

Her dismay turned to outright disbelief as she watched Kerrick bow over the young woman's hand and lead her out onto the ballroom floor. The strains of a waltz were beginning to play. Unable to watch them together, she swung back to face her sister.

Louisa, however, continued to watch them. "Well," she said when she finally spoke, "Nicholas never mentioned this. I had no idea there was anything between Kerrick and Rose Hardwick."

Catherine couldn't bear to stand there and discuss the possibility that Kerrick might have an understanding with another woman and so tried to distract her sister. "Where's Nicholas? I'm surprised he isn't adhered to your side."

Louisa made a small sound of exasperation. "We're

not as bad as that."

"Yes, you are," Catherine said with a fond smile. "But I admit it's refreshing to see amidst all the practical unions of the *ton*."

"What do you know of practical unions?"

Catherine shook her head. "I don't know, not really. It's just that I used to think the upper classes were the lucky ones, but beneath their airs I sense something missing. A hollowness."

Louisa didn't hide her surprise. "You have grown very astute. You are no longer just my little sister but a woman now."

Catherine shrugged. "I'm no different today than I was yesterday."

"No," Louisa said, a smile lifting the corner of her lips. "Of course not. And speaking of Nicholas, here he comes."

IT WAS SOME TIME before he was able to return to Overlea's small party. After his obligatory dance with Rose Hardwick, her parents had made it their mission to monopolize his company. He knew they were sending a signal to all the other parents with daughters of a marriageable age that they had a prior claim on him. One based solely on Lady Worthington's lifelong friendship with Kerrick's mother, but which had no actual basis in reality. The entire situation left him more than a little uncomfortable.

Much as he wanted to, he couldn't outright ignore the Worthingtons or he'd never hear the end of it from his mother, so he had to suffer their company far longer than he would have anyone else who'd made such a presumption. He resolved, however, to have a private conversation with Worthington—and soon—to set the man straight about his misplaced hopes for his daughter's future.

Finally tiring of his less-than-effusive company, Lord Worthington left him for the card room and Lady Worthington turned her attention to one of her friends. Free from their suffocating attention, he scanned the room. Annoyance flared when he saw Catherine Evans speaking to Viscount Thornton.

He'd seen her dancing with him when he'd first arrived and had been surprised at the spark of displeasure he'd felt. Until that moment, he hadn't allowed himself to think about the fact that it was Catherine he'd been looking forward to seeing tonight and not his best friend, Nicholas. Catherine he'd missed.

That wouldn't do.

He'd sought out Nicholas and his new bride and had kept his back to the dancing couples lest he give away his interest in Catherine's movements. When Nicholas had left to fetch a drink for his wife, Louisa casually mentioned that her sister was dancing with Viscount Thornton, and he'd had to work to keep a scowl from his face. He knew very little about Thornton, only that he seemed far too young. The thought had risen, unbidden, that Catherine needed someone older, not a young buck who was little more than an untried youth.

He hadn't forgotten the waltz he'd promised her the previous fall. In fact, he'd been about to invite her to dance when Worthington had interrupted. He stopped to speak with the orchestra conductor before making his way back to her. It was fortunate for Thornton that he had already departed.

"I wasn't sure we'd see you again tonight," Nicholas said, amusement in his gaze. "What's this I hear about there being an understanding between you and Rose Hardwick?"

Nicholas was clearly enjoying himself at his expense. Somehow Kerrick resisted the urge to swear, but he couldn't keep from casting a quick glance at Catherine. She was looking across the room at something, pretending not to be interested in their conversation. By the stiff set of her shoulders, however, he knew that wasn't the case.

"I don't intend to offer for her, if that's what you're wondering."

Nicholas's eyes narrowed. "From Worthington's behavior, it's clear he expects you to."

Kerrick could sense every ear in the near vicinity straining to hear their conversation. Nicholas realized it as well and had kept his voice low.

Kerrick shrugged. "He's a viscount and I'm an earl. He wishes to see his daughter marry well. Of course he hopes for a match."

Nicholas frowned. "You didn't seem inclined to dissuade him from that impression."

He needed to call a halt to this conversation before it became even more uncomfortable. "It's complicated," he said, not wanting to get into the ties that bound their two families. "You can ask me about it later. For now, however, I promised Miss Evans a dance, and I fear she will be put out if I go back on my word."

Catherine smiled up at him, but it didn't quite reach her eyes. Just then the musicians finished their current piece and began to play the next one. He could see her surprise.

"Another waltz?"

"I didn't promise just any dance."

Fool that he was, his heart lightened when her eyes

sparkled with her customary good humor. Thankful that she no longer seemed upset with him, he held out his arm to lead her out. She placed her small hand on his forearm and his heart threatened to soar.

Ignoring the frown that Louisa cast in his direction, he led Catherine to the center of the room. She didn't hesitate for a moment but moved into his arms as though she belonged there. And damn his eyes if it didn't feel as though she did.

He had a feeling his affection for Catherine was going to complicate his friendship with Nicholas and his wife. He'd suspected last fall that Catherine held a *tendre* for him, and the very last thing he wanted was to cause her any hurt. At the same time, he wasn't ready to follow his friend's lead into wedded bliss and would have to make it clear that there could be nothing more than friendship between him and Catherine. Later, though. At the moment he didn't want to think about anything but the delightful young woman in his arms. The one whom, he told himself, he must think of only as a younger sister.

As soon as they started moving, she started talking. Telling him about the events he'd missed, the plays she'd seen. He couldn't help but compare her to Rose Hardwick as he gazed down at her. Both beautiful, but in entirely different ways. Rose's beauty was earthy and obvious while Catherine's beauty was delicate, almost ethereal. Her pale hair was piled high on her head in a complicated arrangement with wispy tendrils that curled around her face and neck. Her skin was creamy smooth and her eyes a vivid shade of blue he recalled only ever seeing on one other person—her brother, John, whom he'd met briefly at Nicholas and Louisa's wedding. Louisa looked very much like Catherine, but her eyes were gray and seemed to reflect her more serious nature.

Looking at Catherine, one could be forgiven for expecting her to be the kind of person who held herself aloof and distant, but she was the exact opposite. She was warm and generous, a discovery that had surprised him at first. When Catherine smiled, she meant it. Her smiles weren't put on for effect, and they certainly weren't pulled out and used as a weapon to charm someone into acquiescing to her latest whim. Not like they were with most of the other women he'd met. Not like Rose Hardwick.

He found himself staring down at her in rapt attention as she recounted the lengths to which many of the young ladies had gone to attract the attention of a much sought-after suitor.

Halfway through one particularly amusing story, she stopped. Her brow furled. "You seem so serious."

"Do I?" He didn't feel that way. "I am trying to picture poor Mildred Markham falling in the Serpentine while trying to capture Lord Beckham's attention. I'm sure he will remember her for quite some time."

She laughed, the sound light and breathy, and he could see that heads nearby turned in their direction. Catherine, however, was oblivious to the interest she attracted.

"I really shouldn't gossip. Their actions are no different than mine."

He raised a brow at that. "You've fallen into the Serpentine while trying to gain someone's attention?"

"Oh no," she said with a firm shake of her head. "I did, however, embarrass myself when I wandered away to look at some of the flowers at Hyde Park last week."

Kerrick remembered Catherine's fondness for plants, particularly exotic ones, but she wouldn't have found anything along Rotten Row to compare with the collection at Overlea Manor. "I fail to see how that could have caused you embarrassment."

"I wandered quite afield and into a small copse of trees. I was fine, of course, but apparently a panic went up when I disappeared and a search party was arranged. Ten lords who were visiting the park deserted their companions to help search for me."

Kerrick couldn't contain his laughter as he pictured the scene. "I find it difficult to believe Louisa or Nicholas would have raised the alarm when they found you'd wandered off."

"You know me too well," she said, affecting an expression of chagrin. "However, I was with Lord Thornton. He doesn't know of my fondness for plants and gardens. We were having a leisurely stroll when he stopped to greet a friend of his. When he realized that I'd disappeared, he assumed I'd been abducted and raised the alarm."

She expected him to laugh, of course. The corners of her mouth had tilted up with unrepentant mirth and it was with great difficulty that he returned her smile. But her admission had wiped away his amusement. Why was he surprised that men were paying her court? Thornton was young and seemed innocuous, but he hated the very thought of the two of them together. They had made a striking pair when they were dancing, with their youth and blond-haired, blue-eyed good looks. Kerrick didn't know Thornton enough to do more than greet him in passing, but he found himself hating the man.

Her head tilted with curiosity when he didn't reply right away, and he knew she was going to prod. Before she could do so, he said, "I hope your experiences so far have lived up to your expectations. I remember how much you were looking forward to your season."

She sighed. The sound seemed so forlorn and unlike her.

"I admit I've been a little bored."

Her admission surprised him. "I don't have much experience with young women entering society, but I don't think I've heard any of them describe the social whirlwind as boring."

"Oh no," she said, rushing to correct him. "Well, not precisely. There is much to do, and I have enjoyed many aspects of life in town, especially the theater. But how many balls and routs can one be expected to attend before they all blend into one another? I only wish…"

When she didn't continue, he prodded. "You only wish…?"

She shook her head. "It's nothing. I've been reading about how the gardens at Richmond Palace and Kew have recently been united, and apparently they've acquired plants from various naval expeditions around the world. Plants that cannot be found anywhere else in England." She sighed again. "I was hoping to visit the gardens, but given Louisa's condition she has been so tired of late and doesn't want to commit to doing that much walking. And I hesitate to ask Nicholas since he spends much of his time these days hovering over my sister. I know he'd hate to be away from her for so long."

It only took him a moment to realize what she was implying. "Louisa is increasing?"

"Oh no," she said, a look of horror on her face. "I wasn't supposed to say anything. It is still very early and they don't wish to announce it yet."

He leaned a little closer as he swept her across the ballroom floor and spoke in a low voice. "Your secret is safe with me." Their eyes caught and held, and Kerrick had the odd sensation that he was drowning in the blue depths of her gaze.

It was then that he noticed the scent she'd chosen to wear. He'd so often seen her at the conservatory during his stay at Overlea Manor that he'd come to associate the scent of tropical flowers with her. Here, though, there could be no attributing her perfume to her surroundings. It was a light scent, yet still exotic and so completely her. It seemed to reach out and envelop him, and for several long moments the rest of the room fell away as he looked down at her.

He gave himself a quick mental shake of his head as he tried to remember what else he'd wanted to say. Oh yes, Kew Gardens. "As for the other, I'd be honored to escort you to the gardens. I even know someone who should be willing to act as your chaperone."

Catherine's face lit with excitement and her obvious joy made him feel as though he were ten feet tall.

"I knew everything would be better with you here."

CATHERINE HAD ALREADY met the Duke of Clarington, a longtime friend of both Nicholas and Kerrick's, and Clarington's new duchess of less than a year. Kerrick wasn't certain how the duchess had accomplished it, but she had managed to turn Clarington's head with relative ease during the past season. At the time, Kerrick had been amused by his friend's torment when she'd seemed to favor another over him, but it had all turned out well in the end, and the two were as happy a couple as Nicholas and Louisa. Which, given the state of most marriages among members of society, was quite an anomaly.

The duke and duchess were deep in conversation with Louisa and Nicholas when they returned from their waltz. The duchess was taller than most of the women present, and her height, coupled with her red hair, made her stand out in any crowd. She was undeniably beautiful, but it was Catherine who held his attention as she informed everyone, with great enthusiasm, of their planned trip to Kew Gardens.

He dragged his gaze away from Catherine, the task

more difficult than he would have previously thought, and turned to the new duchess. "Miss Evans mentioned that Lady Overlea would be unable to join us, so I thought I'd ask you to accompany us. She hoped to visit tomorrow, but we can make arrangements for another day if that would better suit your schedule."

Louisa's relief at not being asked to attend was clear, and he didn't miss the glance the sisters exchanged. No doubt she was wondering if Catherine had told him about her newly expectant state.

"Tomorrow would be perfect," the duchess said. "I've heard the gardens are lovely."

Kerrick ignored the knowing smirk on Clarington's face. He found he was actually looking forward to the outing. Not because he was particularly interested in plants or gardens—he'd never really paid much attention to them—but because it meant he would get to spend more time with Catherine. That thought should have worried him, but it didn't.

"I know I wasn't invited," Clarington said, "but I think I'll join you. Wouldn't want to leave you outnumbered by women." The gleam in his eye spoke of less noble reasons for wanting to join their party, and at that moment Kerrick regretted having teased his friend the previous year when he was finding it hard to resist the duchess's charms.

CHAPTER TWO

KERRICK DISMOUNTED AND handed the reins of his horse to the stable boy waiting outside Overlea's town house. It was just past eleven, and in his quest to ensure Catherine enjoyed her day, he'd already been to Kew and back. He wasn't sure why it was so important to him that he make her happy, but he had no doubt she'd be excited when she learned he'd arranged to have the head gardener himself conduct their tour.

She deserved no less. When he'd stayed at Nicholas's estate the previous fall, Catherine had been a new resident to Overlea Manor. She had taken it upon herself to conduct an inventory of the plants Nicholas's grandmother had collected and displayed at the manor's conservatory. He'd seen firsthand how she would disappear for hours at a time, only surfacing from her quest to catalog the unnamed plants when dinner was announced.

A large, lacquered black carriage bearing Clarington's crest was already stationed outside the house. When he entered, he found everyone gathered in the drawing room. Catherine was seated on the settee next to the duchess, the two deep in conversation. Louisa, looking as though she hadn't slept at all the night before, sat in a chair placed at a right angle to them. Clarington and Overlea were conversing by the window, but it was impossible to miss the concern on the latter's face as he glanced at his wife.

Kerrick accepted everyone's welcome before joining the men. "Nicholas," he said, greeting Overlea by his Christian name. Nicholas had never expected to inherit the title, and having lost both his father and older brother only recently, he preferred to be addressed informally by his close friends.

Kerrick saw the anticipation on Clarington's face when he turned his attention to him. "Behave this afternoon," he said, keeping his voice low so the women wouldn't overhear him.

"Of course." Clarington gave him a calculating look

before adding, "After all, it's the least I can do after you declined to poke fun at me last year about Charlotte every chance you got."

Kerrick swore softly and Clarington laughed with glee. He turned to Nicholas, but his glib plea for sympathy died before the words were spoken. The look on his friend's face almost had him taking a step back.

"You're not courting Catherine," Nicholas said, his voice laced with menace.

Kerrick was speechless, but only for a moment. "Who told you I was? She and I are merely friends."

Nicholas shifted so his back was to the women who, fortunately, hadn't taken note of their heated exchange. "Louisa's worried that Catherine hopes otherwise. You would do well to disabuse her of that notion. Especially since everyone appears to be under the impression that you are all but formally engaged to Worthington's daughter."

A spark of anger, swift and hot, shot through him. "Everyone is wrong," he said, not bothering to hide his annoyance. "Make no mistake, if such a travesty were to happen, you would know about it. You, above all people, should know that I would never take advantage of an innocent—even when others demand I do so."

The flare of annoyance on Nicholas's face told him they were both thinking of what they'd gone through the previous fall when Nicholas had enlisted Kerrick's help. At the time, Nicholas had thought he was suffering from the same illness that had already taken his brother and father, and he had asked Kerrick to father a child with Louisa to keep the marquisate from falling into his unscrupulous cousin's grasp. Kerrick had been reluctant to agree to the plan from the beginning and had decided he wouldn't go through with it when he realized, not long after meeting her, that Louisa was very much in love with her new husband.

It also hadn't taken him long to discover that Nicholas, even though he tried to deny it, very much wanted his wife only for himself. A lesser man would have taken advantage of the opportunity provided by Nicholas's scheme. Louisa was a beautiful woman, after all, and at the time she'd been trapped in a marriage with a man who went to great lengths to distance himself from her. But despite her seeming fragility, Nicholas's wife had a core of steel, and he'd known right away that she wouldn't be swayed by any efforts on his part to seduce her. And he'd respected his friend's feelings too much to even attempt it. He was only glad that everything had worked out in the end.

"What am I missing?" Clarington asked, breaking into the heavy silence.

Nicholas was the first to look away. "Nothing," he said, his jaw tight. "Ancient history."

Kerrick didn't elaborate. One of the reasons Nicholas had chosen to approach him about fathering his heir was the knowledge that Kerrick would take the secret of his insane plan to the grave. Clarington had been away on his honeymoon at the time and hadn't even learned of Nicholas's marriage until the whole situation had been resolved.

"We should go, then. An afternoon of investigating greenery awaits us," Clarington said in an obvious attempt to lighten the atmosphere.

The four who made up their party for the outing exited the house amidst a chorus of good-byes and general chatter. Clarington helped first his wife, then Catherine, into the waiting carriage before following, leaving Kerrick to enter last. When he did, he found himself seated opposite Catherine.

He kept his tone casual as he revealed that the head gardener would lead them through their tour. The look on Catherine's face—a mix of happiness, excitement, anticipation—more than made up for the extra effort he'd already gone through that morning.

CATHERINE COULD BARELY contain her excitement at the prospect of seeing in person many of the plants she'd only seen pictures of in books. She'd found it tedious when, shortly after arriving in London for the start of the season, she'd discovered that every member of the *ton* seemed content to limit their enjoyment of nature to afternoon rides in Hyde Park during the fashionable hour, or to visiting the Vauxhall Pleasure Gardens for its famed evening entertainments. Much to her disappointment, she'd learned that when it came to plant life, there was nothing truly of note in either place.

She only half listened as Clarington informed Kerrick of what he'd missed during his absence from town. She wasn't surprised to discover that men were only too happy to take part in gossiping, though she suspected they would take umbrage at her using that term. They probably considered it *keeping abreast of current events.*

She tried not to stare, but Kerrick was seated directly opposite her and it was only natural for her to look at him. If it were possible, he was even more handsome than when she'd last seen him the previous fall. His dark hair was shorter than she remembered, but she liked the stark haircut on him. The sharp planes of his face were more noticeable now. And how had she forgotten the way his deep blue eyes crinkled when he smiled? Her eyes were drawn again and again to his mouth, and she found herself wondering just what it would feel like to kiss him.

She remembered, again, how he had held her in his strong arms as he'd waltzed with her the night before and indulged in a daydream wherein he'd stopped and, his eyes never leaving hers, pulled her to his chest and kissed her. She couldn't hold back her sigh at the fantasy. Kerrick's gaze swung to her face, and for a moment she had the mortifying notion that he knew what she'd been thinking.

Their eyes met and held. There was something in his she didn't recognize, but it had every nerve in her body tingling with anticipation. Her breath hitched and she found she had to remind herself to continue to breathe. She noticed the way his jaw tightened just before he tore his gaze from hers and turned to face Clarington. The air between them seemed to crackle with a new sense of awareness. At first she thought that increased awareness was only on her part, but the way he seemed to hesitate slightly before turning to look at her whenever she spoke told her that he, too, felt it.

That knowledge was almost enough to make her forget the reason for their trip, but all too soon they arrived at Kew. Kerrick almost leapt from the carriage when it came to a stop outside the main gates. She wasn't sure if she should be insulted by his seeming haste to be out of her presence, but she felt marginally better when he handed her out of the carriage, holding on to her hand a beat too long as he looked down at her. When the duchess gave a delicate little cough, he re-collected himself and released her to assist the other woman.

Clarington appeared to be amused when he stepped down, but Catherine couldn't say why. She didn't miss the frown Kerrick aimed at his friend, though.

"Where should we go first?" the duchess asked.

Kerrick pointed south. "Clifton said we'd find him near the temple of Bellona."

"The Roman goddess of war," Catherine said.

Kerrick didn't hide his surprise. "You know your mythology."

"It probably comes as a great shock to you, but I do know a few things aside from the names of plants."

In response to the mock censure in her voice, Kerrick sketched a formal bow. "I'll have to remember not to underestimate you in future."

The duchess moved to stand next to Catherine and looked at the two men. "It doesn't appear that Mr. Clifton heard our carriage arrive. Why don't the two of you check to see if he's at the temple while Catherine and I wait here to make sure we don't miss him?"

Clarington gave his wife a little salute, which earned

him a light slap on the arm, before the two men headed toward the small building.

Catherine turned to the duchess, who was only a few years older than herself. "I wanted to thank you again, Your Grace, for agreeing to come today. I know most people would find such an outing very dull."

The duchess waved a hand in dismissal. "I'm very glad for the opportunity to get to know you better. Speaking of which, I think we can drop the formalities here. I insist you call me Charlotte when we are away from the inflexibility of society."

"I would like that very much," Catherine said.

"Good. Now that we've settled that matter, tell me about Kerrick and yourself. I can see that you like him."

Catherine wondered if the entire world could tell how much she cared for Kerrick. Nevertheless, she tried to act nonchalant. "He's a friend of Nicholas's and spent some time with us last fall. We became friendly during that time."

Charlotte made a soft tsking sound. "Don't be coy. You know that's not what I meant."

Catherine sighed. "You are correct. However, I don't think he feels the same way about me." She hesitated before sharing a further confidence. "He seemed quite close to Louisa when he visited. I thought he might have feelings for her."

"I'm not sure I believe that," Charlotte said after giving her statement consideration. "From what I've seen, his behavior with her is every bit as friendly but circumspect as his behavior toward me. He's different when he looks at you, though."

Catherine's pulse leaped. "Do you think so? I find it impossible to tell sometimes if a gentleman is just being kind or if there's something more behind that kindness."

"I was in the same predicament just last year."

"You and His Grace?"

Charlotte nodded. "I've known him for years, but I feared he always considered me his sister's annoying friend."

"Surely not." Seeing the way the duke doted on his wife, it was hard to believe he'd ever considered her annoying.

Charlotte nodded with gravity. "I'm afraid so. I made quite a nuisance of myself when I was younger."

"What changed?" Catherine asked, eager to learn how the other woman had finally managed to capture the interest of the man she loved.

"Well, first there were a few years when we didn't see one another, and during that time I grew up. Both in maturity and in physical appearance. You, however," she said, turning a critical eye to Catherine, "are already very beautiful."

"Was that all?" If that was the duchess's secret, her case was truly hopeless. Kerrick was hardly falling all over himself nor writing sonnets composed to her beauty.

Charlotte shook her head. "I followed the conventional wisdom that says men want most that which they cannot have."

At Catherine's obvious confusion, Charlotte smiled. "I made him believe that I was not the least bit interested in him, and then I proceeded to flirt with any man who would give me more than a few moments' notice."

Catherine mulled that advice over in her head. Did she have it in her to fake an attraction where none existed? Her thoughts went to Rose Hardwick. Was that what the other woman was doing? Pretending to be aloof to Kerrick? Rose did surround herself with other admirers. Was she attempting to draw Kerrick's interest by pretending indifference? The thought made her feel slightly ill, because that would mean that Catherine had a direct rival for Kerrick's attention. One who already seemed to hold the advantage if her parents' expectations were any indication.

"I'm not sure I can do that."

"You might not have to," Charlotte said. She must have seen Catherine's confusion, for she added, "Kerrick already likes you very much."

Catherine hesitated a moment before saying, "I've heard there are expectations about his future."

Charlotte looked at her levelly. "Clarington tells me that there is no formal betrothal, and I suppose he would know. I might only be three and twenty, but over the years I've seen that expectations do not always turn into reality. Until Kerrick declares himself and is accepted, he is free to pursue others. Or to be pursued."

The duchess was correct, of course. If there was no formal understanding between the two, and since neither of the parties involved showed any sign of having a romantic attachment for the other, what would it hurt to follow where her heart led? She would never forgive herself if she didn't at least try to capture Kerrick's interest.

"What do I do? I cannot be coy with other men. Not when…" She was unsure of how to continue, but Charlotte knew what she was going to say.

"Not when the rival for his affections is using the same tactic? And doing so splendidly, I might add."

The note of admiration in Charlotte's voice was enough to make Catherine despair.

"You'll have to use the opposite strategy. Since Rose

Hardwick is putting a lot of effort into pushing Kerrick away, we'll have to make sure he's pushed in your direction."

Catherine liked the sound of that. "How?"

Charlotte considered that for several moments. "To begin," she said, "I'll do what I can to keep my husband occupied over the next few weeks. If Kerrick wishes to spend some quality time bonding with a male friend, he'll be forced to do so with Overlea. That should put him into your path more often."

Catherine was so caught up in their conversation that she hadn't noticed that Kerrick and the duke were already returning until the duchess silenced what she was about to say by reaching out to tap her arm and inclining her head to the right. Catherine turned to find them with a middle-aged man of average height whose skin bore witness to the fact that he spent a great deal of time outdoors.

After Kerrick made the introductions, Mr. Clifton smiled at her and said, "I hear you are very fond of plants. What would you like me to show you first?"

"I want to see everything," Catherine said with a self-deprecating laugh. "But I fear my companions wouldn't be too happy to spend the next several hours wandering over every acre of land."

Mr. Clifton's eyes warmed at her obvious

enthusiasm. "I'm afraid that wouldn't be possible, even if they were willing, but I can show you an assortment of what we've collected here."

"Can we start with the plants that have been collected from voyages abroad?"

"You are a woman after my own heart," he said, holding out his arm for her to take.

Over the next three hours, Catherine saw many plants that she'd only seen in black-and-white sketches, and some that she'd never even heard of. Her favorites were the tropical flowers. It was still early spring and many of them weren't yet in bloom, but the assortment of vibrant colors and shapes was enough to make her mind whirl.

More than once she'd exclaimed over something and turned to find Kerrick watching her. At first it was with patient amusement, but then something changed. She couldn't tell what, exactly, and she didn't want to make too much of it lest she build up her hopes only to have them dashed, but there was definitely a new connection between them.

The duchess seemed to be taking her promise to help bring her and Kerrick together seriously and went out of her way to drag her husband off to secluded corners of the various gardens they saw. She didn't think Kerrick or Clarington knew what she was doing, the latter probably thought that the romantic atmosphere of the gardens was behind his wife's desire to spend time with him separate from the rest of the group, but Catherine knew exactly what was afoot and appreciated the duchess's effort.

When they reached the orangery, the last stop on their impromptu tour, even she was starting to flag.

"I would love to return later in the year and see the trees with their oranges," Catherine said with a wistful sigh.

"Unfortunately, the site won't be as impressive as we'd hoped for," Mr. Clifton said. "The trees are starting to show signs of stress because they are not receiving enough light in here. We're going to have to move them somewhere that has more windows. Perhaps even a glass roof. Hopefully they won't decline too much before that can happen."

"I hope not," Catherine said. "That would be such a shame."

She gave the trees one last look before turning back to the others. She was reluctant to leave and made a vow that she would return one day to see more of the gardens.

"What is the matter," she asked when she saw the odd expression on Kerrick's face.

"You have something right here," he said, brushing

a finger across his nose.

She reached up and rubbed her own nose and heard Charlotte's laugh. She turned to look at the duchess, but the woman only gave her a quick wink before dragging her husband and Mr. Clifton away.

"You're just making it worse," he said.

She glanced at her hands and grimaced when she saw the dirt on her gloves.

"Here," he said, removing a handkerchief from his pocket. He was about to hand it to her but hesitated. "If you don't mind?" He held up the square of crisp white cloth.

Catherine shook her head and it was everything she could do to keep her breathing even as he stepped closer and raised the handkerchief to wipe away what she hoped was only a small smudge of dirt. He was impossibly close—closer than he'd been when they'd danced. His brow furrowed in concentration as he rubbed the dirt away from her nose.

When he was done, he didn't step back. Instead, he continued to gaze down at her.

"You're tired," he said.

The look in his eyes, together with the heat inside the orangery, brought a flush to her cheeks.

"And hot," she managed when she remembered to breathe again.

His eyes darkened, and for a moment she found herself thinking that he was going to kiss her. But then he looked away and took a step back, and the moment was shattered.

"We should join the others. They're probably halfway to the carriage by now."

Catherine could only nod in reply as she took his arm and they exited the building.

CHAPTER THREE

HE DREAMT OF Catherine that night. Heated dreams in which he had separated her from the rest of their party and taken her into a maze that existed only in his dream. He awoke feeling frustrated and more than a little guilty. As he lay in bed, his body still hard and his mind clouded with erotic images, his thoughts went to Nicholas's warning to stay away from Catherine. If his friend learned that he was dreaming about divesting his sister-in-law of her clothing and making her take note of something other than the infernal plant life that so interested her, he'd have Kerrick's hide.

But it wasn't just her body that attracted him. If he were merely suffering from sexual frustration, he knew several women who would be more than happy to ease his discomfort. He realized, though, that Catherine Evans was more than just a young woman making her debut in society. She was a contradiction. She seemed so young and innocent at times, and along with that youth came an exuberance that charmed him. But she was also intelligent. She liked gardening, yes, but her interest went beyond merely liking pretty flowers. He'd noticed when he was at Overlea Manor the previous fall that she'd studied with the dedication of a scholar the exotic plants Nicholas's grandmother had collected over the years. She'd spent hours looking through books and making notes of her own. He couldn't fathom why plants held such fascination for her or why she'd devote so much time to their study. He did know from what Overlea had told him that Catherine's quick thinking had saved her sister's life.

Catherine had depths that weren't immediately obvious when one first met her, and he couldn't deny that he longed to explore those hidden layers. Longed to learn just what it was she desired most in life. He realized that he hoped it was him, but he attributed that desire to his vanity. Women made no secret that they found him attractive, and Catherine wasn't immune to his charms. And she had said she was bored before his return to town. If the far-too-young

Viscount Thornton was any indication of the company she'd been keeping, it was no wonder she needed more stimulating companionship.

He shook his head when he realized the direction in which his thoughts were headed. Overlea had been correct in his assumptions the day before. He *did* want to court Catherine. She was younger than him, yes, but only by eleven years. It wasn't unusual for men much older than he to marry someone her age. Normally he preferred the company of more experienced women who only expected a short-term dalliance. There was only one type of relationship he could pursue with Catherine Evans—a more permanent one. And for the first time in his life, he found that the prospect of marriage no longer seemed so disagreeable to him.

But he had one very important matter to attend to before he could even consider the possibility of courting Catherine. He had to clear up the matter of the Worthingtons' expectation that he would one day marry their daughter. He suspected his mother had encouraged them in that belief.

He was considering whether to break the news first to his mother or to Lord Worthington when a knock at his bedroom door brought him out of his musings. When no one entered right after, he knew it wasn't his valet come to dress him for the day. He rose, donned his banyan, and opened the door to find his butler on the other side, a silver tray balanced on one hand. His guilt immediately made him think that Overlea was downstairs at that very moment, ready to pummel him for his wayward thoughts. Hoping he wasn't about to be called out simply for glancing in Catherine's direction, he reached for the calling card placed neatly in the center of the tray.

When he read the name of his visitor, he managed to keep his expression impassive. He offered a curt nod by way of reply, closed the door a little too carefully, and moved to the bellpull to summon his valet. What he really wanted to do, however, was to hit something. His gaze shot to the window, a fleeting thought of escape flickering through his mind, but he repressed the urge with ruthless practicality. Given the failure of his recent line of inquiry, he shouldn't have been surprised to learn that the unofficial representative of the Home Office had seen fit to contact him directly. Escaping now would only delay the inevitable.

The Earl of Brantford waited for him in the library, seated in one of the high-backed wing chairs before the unlit fireplace. As always, the fair-haired man was the picture of lazy indolence. But Kerrick knew he was far from the carefree noble he pretended to be. What had him on high alert, however, was the file Brantford had placed on the small table next to his elbow. Kerrick's day had just taken a marked turn for the worse.

"Brantford," he said by way of greeting as he settled in the chair across from him. "I must say, I'd rather hoped not to see you again so soon."

"Alas, life is filled with disappointment. I'd hoped to be much closer to ending this matter as well, but I recently learned that is not to be."

Annoyance flared, but Kerrick wouldn't allow it to show. It never served to allow one's emotions free rein in this business. "I thought I'd been clear that my last round of queries would be the end of our arrangement."

"How odd. I'd heard that you hadn't turned up any leads." As always, Brantford's tone was even.

"You heard correctly. The trail was already cold when I arrived and I couldn't find anyone who knew anything of import."

Brantford eyed him steadily. "So you haven't, in fact, fulfilled your final duty to the Home Office."

It was with great effort that Kerrick kept his temper in check. "I went on the mission, which was all that was required of me. This meeting is at an end."

He started to stand, but the gleam in Brantford's eye stilled his movement.

"Officially, yes, your term of service has run its

course. However, I believe there was a personal favor you asked of me last fall. I would ask for a favor in return. You are, as you say, not required to oblige me…"

He didn't have to complete the sentence. Kerrick had put himself in the other man's debt when he'd called on him to help Nicholas discover who had been trying to harm his family. Only someone with no honor would ignore a debt.

"This is the last of it," he said.

"Of course."

Kerrick settled back in his chair, resigned to yet another trip. Brantford was doing his best to appear bored, which he knew meant that he wasn't going to like what was coming.

"Where are you sending me?"

"Actually, we're not sending you anywhere. Your services are required right here in town."

Unease settled within him. "Doing what?"

Brantford brushed an imaginary piece of lint from his sleeve, the movement slow and precise, before meeting his gaze. "Worthington has become a person of interest in our attempt to discover who has been leaking sensitive information to the French. It has not escaped our notice that the man has certain expectations of you with respect to his daughter. That places you in the perfect position to observe him more closely."

The words settled over him like a death sentence. He couldn't keep his thoughts from going to the young woman he'd hoped to court a scant few minutes before. If he was obliged to pay court to Rose Hardwick for the rest of the season, that would leave Catherine free to form an attachment elsewhere. Somehow he hid his bitter disappointment.

"And if I don't wish the entire world to believe I'm courting Miss Hardwick?"

Surely he only imagined the flicker of annoyance that crossed Brantford's face, the slight tightening of his jaw before he continued.

"I doubt anyone would consider it a hardship to pay court to a beautiful young woman. You won't be the only man dancing attendance on her. As long as you are careful not to find yourself in a compromising position with her, she will survive the season with her reputation intact. You will then be free to turn your attention back to Miss Evans."

Yes, Brantford was most definitely annoyed if he was baiting him. Kerrick let the comment slide, however. Nothing would be gained by arguing with the man.

"Tell me everything," Kerrick said.

Brantford reached for the file and leaned forward to hand it to him. Kerrick took it but didn't look at its contents.

"What little information we have is in there," Brantford said. "I am afraid it isn't much, which is why we are in need of your assistance."

Kerrick didn't know much about Worthington, but he found it impossible to believe the man was a spy for the French. He didn't have the necessary subtlety for the role.

"Why on earth would anyone believe Worthington is leaking information? Unless I'm mistaken, he doesn't have access to the kind of secrets the French are seeking."

"No, of course not," Brantford said. "We suspect he is but a small player, and in all likelihood doesn't even know what he's entangled himself in. We've noticed, however, that his finances have recently improved. Not by a very large amount, but enough to have us wondering how he could possibly afford to purchase a much larger house in Mayfair. Until recently, his finances were on the verge of collapse."

"Perhaps," Kerrick said with a bitter twist of his lips, "he is just borrowing against the possibility of his daughter marrying well."

Brantford shook his head. "We've already made a

few discreet inquires and have confirmed that his finances have improved. Not so much that he doesn't wish to align his family with yours, of course, but enough that he no longer needs to worry about creditors taking everything that isn't entailed. The same could not be said six months ago."

"You believe there's someone else."

"Yes. Worthington is now comfortable, but his cash flow has not increased so much that we believe he's selling secrets directly to the French. But he does have friends placed highly in the navy. We believe he is telling someone else what he knows about the movements of our naval fleet. When we learn with whom he's been speaking, we expect to discover who has been keeping Napoleon well informed of Britain's plans in a number of areas. Have a look at the file and you'll see why we're convinced we finally have a lead on discovering the traitor."

Kerrick rose to his feet and Brantford did the same. "I'll keep you advised of my findings."

Was that sympathy on the other man's face?

"We wouldn't ask this of you if we weren't convinced of Worthington's involvement."

"Of course," Kerrick said, his heart already beginning to turn cold in anticipation of the ruse he was about to enact.

CHAPTER FOUR

Catherine was on top of the world. The outing to the gardens at Kew the day before could not have been more perfect. The beauty of the gardens had surpassed her imaginings—she had never thought to see such an array of exotic plants in her life. But she had to admit even they had not been the highlight of her day. No, yesterday had been perfect because she had spent most of it in Lord Kerrick's company.

Unlike the other men who merely tolerated her interest in gardening, Kerrick seemed to have been engaged. Oh, he'd been feigning at first, that much was obvious to everyone present. She didn't know what had changed, but after a while it seemed as though her enthusiasm had been contagious. And when he'd mentioned improving the gardens at his own estate, she couldn't help but imagine what it would be like to have control over that endeavor as the lady of the house.

Something else had changed during their visit. She'd begun to believe that he no longer saw her as just his friend's young sister-in-law, but a woman worthy of notice in her own right.

It came as a shock, therefore, to learn only an hour before dinner that he had sent her sister a note to say he would not be able to attend the small dinner party Louisa and Nicholas had planned for that evening. She cornered Louisa in her bedroom as her sister prepared for the evening. Her maid was just adding the final touches to Louisa's simple yet elegant hairstyle.

Catherine didn't wait for her to finish before stating, "Nicholas told me Kerrick isn't coming." She couldn't keep the disappointment from her voice.

"It's to be expected," Louisa said in a tone that was clearly meant to soothe her. "Lord Kerrick has outside concerns that often lead him to change his plans at a moment's notice."

Catherine's curiosity was piqued. "What type of concerns?"

Louisa was silent for a moment and Catherine suspected she was considering whether to tell her the truth. "I shouldn't have said anything. Just know that I am sure he had a very good reason for declining our invitation on such short notice."

She was torn between irritation and resignation at her sister's reply. Louisa was eight years her elder and at times still treated her as a child that needed to be protected. She waited while the maid finished, her impatience growing by the second.

Her sister dismissed the maid after a few minutes and stood to face her, by which time Catherine's emotions had clearly settled on irritation.

"You seem to have forgotten with whom you're speaking. After such a mysterious comment, surely you don't expect me to just shrug my shoulders and carry on as though you've said nothing."

Louisa gave her head a slight shake. "I'd hoped you could leave the matter alone, but it's clear that is not about to happen."

"I am not a child, Louisa. You must stop treating me as one. I'm in town searching for a husband, after all. You seem not to have learned anything after what happened when John left."

Her sister flinched at the accusation and Catherine felt a pang of remorse for having reminded her of the conditions under which their brother had left them before enlisting in the army.

"I'm sorry," she said, reaching out to clasp Louisa's hand and giving it a gentle squeeze. "That was uncalled for."

"Yet unfailingly accurate."

Catherine didn't deny it. They both knew it was the truth. Having lost their mother soon after Catherine's birth and being so much older than her and John, Louisa had always trod a fine line between acting like a sister and an overprotective mother.

"I know you have a particular interest in Kerrick. I'd hoped it was just a youthful infatuation when you met last year and that you'd forget him when your season started and you met other men closer to your own age. But I see that hasn't happened."

"Kerrick is only eleven years older than me. Just last night I heard that Lord Hendricks is looking for a new wife, and he's at least in his fifties." She shuddered. "I pity the poor girl who will no doubt be forced by her parents into that union."

Louisa looked away for several moments and then let out a resigned sigh. With that small exhalation, Catherine knew she had won. Louisa sat, again, in the chair before her dressing mirror, but this time she'd turned so she faced her. Catherine sat on the edge of her sister's bed and waited.

For what, she wasn't certain, but given the grave

expression on her sister's face, her curiosity began to take a darker turn. After their outing the day before, she'd almost forgotten about that little scene between Kerrick and the Worthingtons. And about how he had left her to dance with Rose Hardwick first.

Dread began to rise within her. Surely her sister wasn't about to tell her that Kerrick was courting Rose.

"Tell me, Louisa," she said when she could no longer stand the silence.

The startled expression on her sister's face told her that what had seemed an eternity to her had likely been only a few moments.

"Do you remember last fall, before we learned what was happening with Nicholas, that Lord Kerrick had returned to London?"

Catherine wanted to scream as the suspicion began to take firm hold that her dream of a future with Kerrick was about to be crushed. She managed a wordless nod.

"Kerrick had certain connections he was able to call upon to help uncover what was happening at the time. He'd returned to town to ask for assistance from one of those connections."

Her stomach began to unclench as she realized this had nothing to do with the Worthingtons. "He returned with the Earl of Brantford."

Louisa winced at the name. "Yes, he did. The Earl's presence was a surprise to Nicholas, but he's come to realize that Brantford is not all that he seems."

Catherine frowned, now completely confused. "What does Brantford have to do with all this?"

Louisa shook her head. "I am being silly. If I'm to tell you what I know, which I admit is not much, I should be direct. What I'm about to reveal isn't generally known, and you must promise not to repeat it." She paused, but at Catherine's vigorous nod she took a deep breath and continued. "Brantford works for the Home Office, gathering intelligence for the government."

"Intelligence?"

"He is a spy. Or at least we believe that's what he does. Nicholas has never spoken to him about it. And even if his suspicion is correct, Brantford would never admit to it."

While her sister's revelation came as a surprise, she wasn't sure why her sister was telling her about the Earl of Brantford's secrets.

"And?"

"And Nicholas believes that Kerrick might be one as well."

That was the very last thing she'd expected to hear. "A spy?" Her mind went momentarily blank as she tried to take in this new piece of information.

Kerrick was a spy. A thrill of excitement spread through her after the initial shock had faded. He was certainly handsome enough for the role, and she knew firsthand that he had the charisma someone in such a position would need.

"Catherine!" Louisa's voice broke into her thoughts and her annoyance was plain to see. "This isn't a romantic novel. This is real life, and being a…" She waved her hand, obviously not willing to say the word again. "Well, it's dangerous." She frowned. "Or I suppose it could be. Nicholas told me that Kerrick regularly disappears, sometimes for months at a time, and no one knows what he is doing during that time."

"Of course not," she said, trying, but failing, to keep her true emotions hidden. "You are right, this is quite serious."

Louisa looked toward the heavens, as though for strength, before meeting her eyes again. "I didn't tell you this to engage your romantic sensibilities. I don't know what Kerrick does, but it's possible he could be engaged in work that puts his life in danger. You should look to someone more appropriate."

"More boring, you mean."

"No," Louisa said, the word drawn out to indicate her displeasure. "Someone who might not disappear, never to return."

She couldn't help but smile at her sister's announcement. "Not too long ago you believed Nicholas had an illness that would soon lead to his death."

It was several moments before her sister replied, and the anguish on her face was clear to see. "Yes, I did. But I didn't know of his condition when we married."

Catherine crossed the distance that separated them, kneeled at her sister's feet, and took hold of her hands.

"And if you had known? Would you not still have married him?"

Louisa closed her eyes. When she opened them again she could only nod.

"You see," Catherine said. "These things have a way of working out. I am sure the same will happen for Kerrick and me."

ALMACK'S. HELL. JUST the year before he'd been poking fun at Clarington for his attendance at the annual London marriage mart, and now here he was, playing the part of a man courting the woman all of society assumed would be his future bride.

His arrival did not go unremarked. He'd already decided to play into everyone's expectations. The sooner he learned the truth about Worthington, the sooner he could distance himself from the man's daughter. He felt a twinge of guilt for having to deceive her, but he doubted that any one man could claim her heart.

She had just finished her current set and was making her way back to her mother's side. In moments, the young man who had partnered with her was shouldered out of the way by the group of men that seemed to follow her everywhere. She tossed her head back and laughed gaily, reveling in the attention.

Kerrick refused to be just another member of that group. Fortunately—or unfortunately, as the case may be—her mother went out of her way to scatter Rose's entourage. He wasn't quite sure how she accomplished it, but when he reached them, the coterie of young men was gone.

"Lady Worthington," he said with a slight bow before turning to greet the object of his deception. "Miss Hardwick. You are lovely tonight, as always."

And she was. Her hair was swept up into some complicated arrangement, with several curls left to frame her pale, rosy-cheeked complexion. She wore a dress of demure white, but it was impossible to overlook her obvious bounty. And her eyes shone with amusement, as though she were sharing a private joke with him. He could understand why all those young pups sought her favor. It would make things easier if he shared their enthusiasm for his task of wooing her. His mother would certainly be happy if a match was made between him and the daughter of her good friend. It was almost impossible, however, to keep his thoughts from drifting to another whose beauty was far different, but no less affecting, than that of the young woman before him.

"Lord Kerrick," she said, dipping into an abbreviated curtsy.

"How glad we are to see you here tonight," Lady Worthington said. "We didn't know whether to expect you."

"With such a fine inducement as your daughter, I could hardly keep away," he replied smoothly.

The compliment earned him a look of smugness from Lady Worthington. Rose, however, appeared less than impressed. Given the compliments she normally received, he knew his would be mild in comparison. But he wasn't up to playing the role of besotted fool. He wasn't that good an actor.

He smiled down at Rose. "I hope you thought to save a dance for me tonight."

She aimed a frown of dismay at him. "I'm not sure," she said. "I've have had so many invitations."

Lady Worthington's gasp was almost comic.

"Nonsense, Rose," she said, falling just short of stumbling over her words. "In fact, didn't you say your next dance was free?"

Considering Kerrick could spy a young man standing just at the periphery of his vision, shooting daggers at him with his glare, he recognized the statement for the blatant lie it was. If he hadn't been so put out about being asked to play this ridiculous role, he would have found the entire situation amusing.

"I'd consider myself the most fortunate of men, then, if you'd consent to dance with me."

For a moment he thought Rose was going to deny him, and he realized she didn't want to go through with this charade any more than he did. A reproving look from her mother, however, had Rose inclining her head in acceptance and placing her hand in his.

He thought the look of triumph he aimed at the now-glowering suitor was a nice touch. That look was almost wiped off his face when he turned and saw the Earl of Standish leading Catherine Evans to the ballroom floor. Standish liked his women young, fair, and beautiful, and Catherine was all three. What she wasn't, however, was easy, but that had never before stopped the man.

He kept his expression of good humor firmly in place, but he wasn't about to allow Catherine to fall victim to Standish's less-than-honorable intentions. To that end, he made sure that he and Rose were in the same set as Catherine and her partner. As they moved through the figures of the dance, he divided his attention between his own partner and Standish. The dance was familiar and didn't require much of his attention, but he had to be careful that others in their set didn't notice his distraction. It wouldn't do for everyone to see that he was more interested in Lord Standish than in Rose Hardwick. But what took the most effort was keeping his gaze from seeking out Catherine's slim form as she moved gracefully among the other dancers.

He struggled to keep his temper in check every time he saw Standish bestow his smug smile upon her, and he thought he'd managed it well enough. But his control snapped when the dance came to a close and he saw the other man standing too close to Catherine, his head bent low as he murmured something in her ear. She actually blushed, then laughed before giving his arm a friendly pat. When Standish stepped back, that smug smile firmly in place, Kerrick wanted nothing more than to smash his fist into the other man's face.

He turned his attention back to Rose, and when he saw the speculation in her eyes he feared he had ruined his supposed courtship before it had even begun. He heaved an inner sigh of relief when she brightened again and gazed up at him with the same flirtatious smile he'd seen her give countless other men. He would have to be more careful in future to ensure he didn't betray his feelings.

He tucked her hand into the crook of his elbow and started to walk her back to her mother, all the while hating that he'd turned his back on Catherine and Standish. They'd only taken a few steps when another of Rose's many admirers intercepted them. He was only too happy to hand her over, but he had the presence of mind to affect the appearance of one who was annoyed. He moved off to the side and forced himself to converse with one of his acquaintances.

A few minutes passed before he felt it was safe to search out where Catherine had gotten to. He was relieved to find she was now with her sister and the Duchess of Clarington. He thought about approaching her to ask for a dance, recognizing that it would be better for both their sakes if he kept his distance, but knowing that he wouldn't be able to pull off such a feat. Not if Standish had taken an interest in her.

He had to warn her about him. Catherine wasn't like many of the foolish young women present, but she was still far too innocent to risk wading into those shark-infested waters. The fact that she now had her brother-in-law to watch out for her didn't comfort him. For his own peace of mind, he had to make sure Catherine wouldn't be the next young woman to fall victim to Standish.

When he saw her start, alone, for the door that led to the hallway, he followed at a discreet distance. Talking to her in private would be infinitely better than trying to snatch a few words here and there as they made their way through the figures of another seemingly endless dance.

He followed as she made her way to the ladies' retiring room, seeking out an empty room where he could wait for her. Five minutes later, he was relieved to see her alone when she came back down the hallway. When he stepped from the shadowy doorway, she started. She was about to speak and he raised a finger to his lips to silence her. He slipped back into the room without a word. When Catherine followed, he closed the door behind her.

He turned to face her and found her standing a little too close for his comfort. The room, which appeared to be a sitting room, was dim, the only light provided by the full moon shining through the windows. Nevertheless, he could see the expectant look on her face as she stood there silently, waiting for him to tell her why he'd arranged this meeting. It was with great effort that he broke their eye contact and moved to stand closer to the windows.

Her shoulders lifted in what he assumed was a soft sigh as she followed him. This time, she kept a more respectable distance between them when she stopped.

"I assume this isn't a romantic assignation?"

The images that sprang to mind were swift and vivid, and he had to look away as he worked to dispel them. He recognized his mistake when her scent seemed to reach out and caress him.

He met her curious gaze as he replied. "I wanted to warn you about Standish."

She frowned, a little crease appearing between her eyebrows. "Lord Standish? Why would you warn me about him?"

He realized his fists were clenched at his sides and relaxed them as he spoke. "The two of you were dancing."

Her head tilted to the side, her expression baffled. "And you were dancing with Rose Hardwick."

He had to work to keep from raising his voice. "You shouldn't be dancing with him."

"Whyever not? I have danced with more men tonight than I care to remember. Dancing with Lord Standish meant no more to me than a few minutes of vigorous activity followed by a few pleasant words."

He almost growled as his mind came alive with images of other vigorous activities that were far less innocent.

"Standish consumes girls like you, then tosses them aside when he is done. You need to stay away from him."

She shook her head and closed the distance between them. She stopped a mere foot away. "You're being ridiculous. I was in a crowded room where nothing untoward could have happened."

"I realize that," he said, his tone sharp with annoyance that she wasn't taking his warning seriously. "But it is an acquaintance you shouldn't pursue. With familiarity, he will begin to take other liberties with you." *How could he not?* he added silently.

A spark of anger lit her eyes. "Is that the reason you brought me here?"

"You need to be careful," he said, not sure why she was taking offense when his intention was to safeguard her well-being.

She took another step closer, and now she was near enough that he could see the tiny flecks of gold in her blue eyes. His throat went dry.

"You are not my father," she said, stabbing a finger against his chest in anger. "Nicholas and Louisa are doing a fine job of suffocating me and making sure no one comes too close. I don't need you treating me like a child as well." She gave him another little jab.

Her cheeks were flushed now, her breasts rising and falling with her anger. His gaze flickered downward before he managed to drag his eyes back up to her face.

"I do not see you as a child. And God only knows, I wouldn't describe my feelings for you as *fatherly*." The notion was the furthest thing from the truth.

She seemed to take his admission as a challenge, raising her chin and moving another step closer. Instead of poking at him, she spread her fingers and pressed her whole hand against his chest, just over where his heart was now beating an unsteady rhythm. They were so close it would take no effort at all to lean down and kiss her. His gaze was on her lips and he was imagining how their soft plumpness would feel under his when she spoke.

"How would you characterize your feelings for me?" The words were low, almost breathless.

She swayed toward him. He didn't curb his curse as he moved away from her.

Her hand dropped to her side and her shoulders stiffened. The softness he'd seen in her expression was gone. When she spoke, her words were laced with disappointment. "I should return before someone notices our absence and comes to the incorrect conclusion."

She turned to leave, and almost before he realized he'd moved, he reached out to stop her, wrapping his gloved hand around her bare arm. They both froze at the contact. Slowly, she turned to face him.

"Was there something else you wished to discuss with me?"

"Yes… No… damn it."

He was teetering on the very edge of sanity and Catherine was likely to push him over. He pulled her to him and took her mouth in a scorching kiss that held more than a hint of desperation.

From the way she stiffened at first, he knew he'd surprised her, but he was unable to contain the sense of urgency driving him onward. Within moments, her arms came up to encircle his neck and she pressed herself against him. He couldn't hold back his groan of desire at the feel of her seemingly delicate but surprisingly firm body molded against his. She opened her mouth wider, allowing him to explore its depths. It wasn't long before she began to reciprocate in earnest.

She threaded her fingers through the hair at the nape of his neck, holding his head in place. When her tongue stroked against his, he almost came undone. He wanted… no, he *needed* more. His hands moved down to her bottom and he drew her firmly against him. A soft knock at the door intruded on the haze of desire clouding his mind.

He pushed away from her. Her eyes were still closed and she swayed toward him, but he gave her shoulders a small shake. Her eyes opened with great slowness and she looked up at him in dazed wonder.

He cursed silently, wanting nothing more than to draw her back into his arms. Instead, he stepped away from her completely. She frowned but rallied quickly when she heard the second knock. When the door opened and Louisa entered a few seconds later, Catherine was seated sedately on a chair and he was standing by the window.

Kerrick started to speak, but Louisa lifted a hand to stop him.

"I don't want to know." She turned to her sister. "You should return to the ballroom. And you should both consider yourselves fortunate that it is I and not my husband who found you alone in here."

Catherine chose, wisely in his estimation, to remain silent as she made her way from the room without a backward glance.

Louisa followed but halted just inside the door. "I am moving forward on the assumption that you are the same man I knew last fall who wouldn't take advantage of a young woman. And because you were so instrumental in helping my husband and me during that time, I won't speak of this to Nicholas. Please don't give me reason to regret my decision."

She exited from the room then, but her parting words left him feeling the worst sort of cad.

CHAPTER FIVE

SEVERAL DAYS HAD passed since Kerrick kissed her. Catherine had expected that moment to herald a change in their relationship, but if anything, he was more elusive than ever. He hadn't come over to the house since that night and had declined another invitation to dinner.

She was more than a little tempted to march to his town house and demand he tell her whether he had any feelings for her at all. She hated the uncertainty. One moment she was certain that he must care for her, even a little, but the next she remembered how close he and Louisa had been the previous fall. With the latter came the dark fear that when he'd kissed her, he'd seen her only as a substitute for the sister he couldn't have.

Maybe one day she'd have the bravado for such an action, but that day hadn't yet arrived. That was why she'd made sure her sister accepted the invitation to the musicale the Worthingtons were hosting. If Kerrick was courting Rose Hardwick, as rumor would have her believe, he was certain to be there. And if the rumors were true, she needed to see it with her own eyes.

It was with a mixture of determination and trepidation that Catherine stepped across the Worthingtons' threshold that evening with her sister and brother-in-law. The house was overflowing with guests, but she saw Kerrick almost immediately. He stood next to Rose Hardwick and her mother, smiling down at the former. Catherine's stomach clenched. She wanted to turn around and escape before he saw her, but Nicholas ushered Louisa toward the group and she had no recourse but to follow. She plastered a false smile on her face and greeted her hostess before turning her attention to Rose and finally to Kerrick. His smile was carefree as he greeted her with polite courtesy. He acted as though their kiss had never happened, and Catherine could feel the slim thread of hope to which she held begin to unravel.

As the group continued to converse easily, Catherine made her excuses and turned to move away.

Louisa's expression held a hint of concern, but she didn't try to stop her. Catherine didn't care where she headed. She only knew that she needed to distance herself from the striking image of Kerrick standing next to the very beautiful Rose Hardwick as though he belonged at her side.

She'd only moved a few feet, however, when the sound of her name being called brought her to a halt. She turned and stiffened when she saw that her rival for Kerrick's affection had followed her.

"I'm glad you came," Rose said. "We haven't had the chance to come to know one another, but I hope to change that."

If Rose had an ulterior motive for seeking her out, Catherine could detect no sign of it on her face. Instead of gloating, as she would have expected, she saw only honesty.

"I would like that very much." Catherine said the words automatically, as politeness dictated, but didn't mean them. The very last thing she wanted was to befriend her rival for Kerrick's affections.

Rose must have seen her reticence, for her smile faded. She darted a glance over Catherine's shoulder before saying, "I see someone I must speak to. Again, thank you for coming and perhaps we can speak later."

She moved off and Catherine released her breath

with a relieved sigh. She couldn't resist glancing back at Kerrick and saw his gaze shifting away from her. She realized he'd witnessed their brief exchange and wondered if he'd been watching her or Rose. The thought that he sought out the other woman when she wasn't with him depressed her even further.

Time seemed to drag as she greeted people she'd met during her time in London and engaged in social niceties that meant very little. Louisa and Nicholas had found her again not long after she'd torn herself away from having to witness Kerrick fawning over another woman, and together they made their way to the modest-sized ballroom. The room had been converted into a small theater for the evening's entertainment. Catherine shouldn't have been surprised but was at the number of chairs spread out in front of a grand pianoforte. She had no idea how Rose could perform in front of so many people.

She was only human, and while she didn't like the idea of anyone embarrassing themselves in front of such a large audience, she found herself hoping that the Worthingtons' opinion of their only child's talents was vastly overrated. But of course, that proved not to be the case. Catherine's own musical talents were modest, but she recognized true talent when she heard it. And Rose Hardwick had talent in abundance. Her skill on the pianoforte was unquestionable. And her singing... Catherine really wanted to hate her, but her thoughts kept drifting back to Rose's overture of friendship and instead of hate, what she felt was guilt.

Needing to know if Rose's performance was affecting him, Catherine's gaze kept drifting to where Kerrick sat at the back of the room, off to her left. She wondered why he'd taken a seat so far away, and that curiosity only grew when she saw him stand and drift away from the room at precisely the same moment that the Earl of Brantford rose to make a request of Rose. Everyone's attention was on the two of them at the front of the room, especially when the request appeared to throw Rose off-balance. The room itself seemed to hold its breath before releasing it again when Rose started the first strains of the piece Brantford had requested.

Catherine was certain no one had noticed Kerrick's departure. What really had her curiosity at a fever pitch, though, was the fact that he did not return until Rose's performance was almost over a quarter of an hour later.

Rose performed one last song—an ode to lost love that had Catherine gritting her teeth. The applause was enthusiastic and Catherine joined in. She wasn't so stingy as not to give the other woman her due.

Rose had performed for almost half an hour, and when she stepped away from the small dais on which the pianoforte stood, two of her cousins took her place. Their portion of the evening's entertainment only lasted about ten minutes and left no one in doubt that the musicale had been organized to showcase Rose's talent.

She, Louisa, and Nicholas were waiting their turn to speak to Rose and her beaming parents before taking their leave for the night when Kerrick approached their group. He turned to her last. His eyes were warm when they met hers, and she felt the weight of that regard straight through to her toes.

"Miss Evans," he said simply, inclining his head in greeting. They were surrounded on all sides by a crush of people, but everyone seemed to fall away as their gazes locked.

"Lord Kerrick," she replied, looking away and breaking his spell. Conscious again of all the people around them, not the least of whom were her sister and brother-in-law, she tried to keep her own greeting formal. But she failed, and his name came out instead in a breathless whisper.

"Miss Hardwick is very accomplished," Louisa said, drawing his attention away.

"Yes," Nicholas added. "This was quite an endeavor,

organized no doubt for your benefit."

Kerrick shrugged, the movement almost too casual. "Her talent is great. I find it difficult to choose a favorite piece." He turned to her. "What say you, Catherine?"

Catherine wondered at his comment since, as far as she could tell, he had been out of the room for much of the performance. Clearly, he didn't want anyone else to know that, so she answered honestly. "They were all good, but my favorite was the last song. Unrequited love is always so tragic, and the emotion in her voice when she sang actually brought a tear to my eye."

An uncomfortable silence followed her pronouncement, and no one said anything for several long seconds. Kerrick's eyes had narrowed on her as she spoke, an emotion in their depths that she found impossible to name.

Louisa broke the silence again. "Well, my favorite was the Mozart." She sighed. "I never imagined that playing with such proficiency could take such an emotional toll on someone. The poor girl looks quite wrung out."

Catherine followed her gaze and saw that the Earl of Brantford was speaking to the Worthingtons now. Rose did, indeed, look slightly ill. It was all the more startling because she was normally so vivacious.

Perhaps she had been suffering with nerves before the performance after all, and the strain of keeping them under control was only now beginning to show. She felt another stab of guilt as she remembered how she'd rebuffed the other woman's offer of friendship.

Her eyes narrowed as they settled on Brantford. Louisa had told her that he was a spy, but it hardly seemed possible. The man looked to be about Kerrick's age, perhaps a few years older. His hair was fair and cut very short. His demeanor, however, was that of someone who was extremely bored with his surroundings. Whereas Kerrick always seemed to be aware of everything and everyone around him, Brantford acted as though they were all beneath his notice.

Her gaze moved from Brantford to Kerrick and back again as she tried to imagine the two men working together to uncover secrets others wished to keep hidden. As she did so, the pieces of a puzzle seemed to click together in her mind. Brantford and Kerrick were both spies. The former had provided a distraction while the latter slipped away when no one else was paying attention to him. That could only mean Kerrick had been looking for something that evening. Did it have to do with the Worthingtons or was the evening's location merely incidental? Had Kerrick left the room to meet with someone while everyone else was occupied?

When she turned again to look at Lord Kerrick, his eyes were on her. He hadn't missed her examination of Lord Brantford, and at that moment she would give almost anything to know what he was thinking. Did he realize she knew about the service he and Brantford performed for their country? Did he even know that Nicholas and Louisa had guessed he was a spy? Or perhaps he thought she found Brantford attractive. If the latter thought caused him any concern, she hoped it was the reason for his close scrutiny. She smiled brightly at Kerrick before turning back to make small talk with Louisa, but in the back of her mind she was formulating a plan.

His SEARCH THAT evening had proved fruitless. He wasn't sure what he'd expected to find in Worthington's study, but he'd hoped to stumble upon something—anything—that would bring him closer to ending this inconvenient investigation. Correspondence, perhaps, or even a name scribbled on a piece of paper. It had been risky slipping away from the performance to do a quick sweep of Worthington's papers, but he'd had to chance it. He hadn't had enough time to do a thorough search, however, and frustration had weighed heavily on him when he realized he'd already been away too long.

Seeing Catherine again had renewed his determination to put this whole matter behind him. He'd been successful in avoiding her for the past few days, but that had also meant avoiding the various evening entertainments Rose Hardwick had attended. He'd sought out other opportunities to engage Worthington during that time. They were both members of White's, but despite the fact he'd all but haunted the gentleman's club on St. James Street, he hadn't run into the man once.

He'd hoped to accomplish much that night when he accepted the invitation to the musicale. As Nicholas had suggested, he had little doubt that it had been held for his benefit. An effort on her parents' part to showcase Rose's many talents. The way Worthington and his wife had fallen on him when he'd arrived, as though he were the answer to every last one of their prayers, had almost been more than he could bear. He'd accepted their fawning as a necessary evil, hoping to find an opportunity to investigate. Brantford had supplied the distraction that had allowed him to leave the room, and it had been an easy task to slip back in and join the group of men standing near the back of the room. But in the end, the only thing he'd accomplished that evening was to make Worthington believe that a union between Kerrick and his daughter was all but certain.

How he'd ferret out Worthington's guilt was anyone's guess. He was beginning to think the man was innocent and his efforts an exercise in futility.

Something in Catherine's expression after the performance had concerned him when he'd seen her watching Brantford. He couldn't help thinking that she'd somehow seen through the other man's pretense. Of course, Kerrick had involved Brantford in that matter concerning Overlea the previous fall, but he'd been sure to tell her Brantford was merely a friend. It wasn't possible that she'd discovered that the perpetually bored earl had a set of skills that made him very dangerous to his enemies.

He forced his thoughts away from Catherine and back to the task at hand. His investigation had so far had turned up nothing, and he was no closer to ending it than when Brantford had approached him. And so, desperate to find something concrete either way about Worthington's guilt or innocence, he left the man's home as soon as politeness allowed and made a quick trip home. When he went out again, he was dressed appropriately for a visit to the more seedy parts of London. It was time for him to call in a favor and arrange to have Worthington followed.

CHAPTER SIX

CATHERINE WAITED FOR Kerrick a few houses down the street from his town house, the shadow of a tree obscuring her cloaked figure. It hadn't taken her long to find the address in Nicholas's study after he and Louisa had gone to bed. She'd been relieved to discover that Kerrick's house was but a few minutes' walk away.

She knew that what she was doing was foolish and more than a little dangerous, but she was no longer content to sit back and wonder where she stood with Kerrick. After he had kissed her, she'd been so certain he felt something for her, something that went beyond mere fondness. But when she'd seen him tonight, it wasn't difficult to believe that the rumors about him and Rose Hardwick were true. Only… he'd slipped out during Rose's performance and lied about it.

She couldn't play the coquette, pretending an indifference she didn't feel as Charlotte had advised. Or rather, she didn't want to. And so she'd decided she must approach him directly. She was weary of waiting to catch a few glimpses of him every evening only to be disappointed when he didn't show. And when he did, he was still careful to avoid her.

Just that morning she never would have imagined herself brave enough to confront him in this way, but she could no longer bear the uncertainty. Her mind swam with questions that demanded answers. She risked outright rejection, but she had to know how he felt. And to learn the truth, she needed to speak to him alone when no one would interrupt them.

She'd overheard Kerrick telling Nicholas that he planned to go to his club after the musicale, and so she'd sent her maid—after giving her a very hefty bonus so she wouldn't reveal what Catherine was doing—to keep watch over Kerrick's house. She hadn't been certain if the young woman would do as she'd asked or report her actions to the housekeeper. But Catherine had taken the risk, knowing Lily was sending most of her regular pay back to her family to help support them. Fortunately, her gamble had paid off.

When she arrived to take over the watch, Lily told her that Lord Kerrick had been at home when she'd arrived but had left again shortly afterward and had not yet returned. Lily was reluctant to leave her side, but Catherine had promised her another bonus. The fact that she agreed was testament to how much Kerrick was liked. If Catherine had been visiting any other man, she doubted any amount of money would have sufficed to pry her maid from her side.

An hour passed and she started to regret the impulsive decision that had led her out of the house on that warm spring night. The night was still and dark, the only sounds those of the occasional horse and carriage on a not-too-distant street.

She heard footsteps before she saw the figure of a man making his way down the street. It was too dark to tell if it was Kerrick, so she waited, pressed up against the sturdy trunk of the tree, her heartbeat an echo in her ears.

The precariousness of her situation hadn't occurred to her until that moment. Despite the shadow of the tree and the dark cloak that obscured her, she would be seen if he continued past Kerrick's house and glanced in her direction. She should have taken greater care in choosing a hiding spot, but it was now too late.

Her heartbeat quickened, then leapt when the man turned and started up the steps of Kerrick's town house.

"Kerrick," she called, stepping out from the shadow of the tree.

Her voice hadn't been more than an exhalation, but he heard it. His head snapped around and his gaze fell on her. He shook his head in disbelief.

"Tell me I'm losing my mind and that you're not actually standing there."

Something in his expression told her that she hadn't made a mistake.

She pushed back the hood of her cloak. "You're not losing your mind."

He looked up and down the street, then jerked his head toward the side of the house. She met him there by a side door, concealed in the shadows between his house and his neighbor's. He didn't speak again as he unlocked the door and led her inside. The room they entered was unlit, and it took her a few moments to realize they were in the kitchen.

He took hold of her hand and awareness swept through her when she realized that, like her, he wasn't wearing gloves. She remained silent as she followed him up a small staircase and down a short corridor. He led her into another dark room and closed the door firmly behind them before releasing her and stepping away. She heard the sound of a match, followed by the sudden flicker of flame as he bent to light a lamp. She saw then that they were in his study.

The tension in the room, already heavy with what lay unspoken between them, only increased when he straightened and turned to face her. She'd hoped he would admit that he was pleased to see her, but the expression on his face told her he wouldn't make such an admission easily. A muscle flexed along his jaw as he held her with his gaze for several seconds.

"What were you thinking coming here, on your own, at"—his gaze swept to the clock on his desk before returning to hers—"at two in the morning. What if someone had seen you? Your reputation would be in tatters." He shook his head and gave a dry, humorless laugh. "Beyond that, being alone on the streets in the middle of the night is not a safe place for any woman. But one as beautiful as you…"

She went to him then, wanting only to ease his worry. She reached to take hold of his hands but froze when he stepped back to avoid her touch. Her arms dropped to her sides.

"It wasn't far and I took great care not to be seen."

His mouth firmed in a solid line and he seemed to struggle for words. It occurred to her that he didn't want to ask her why she'd come. Well, if he hoped to avoid the subject of what was between them, she was not going to allow that to happen.

"You haven't asked me why I was waiting for you."

"I have no notion what could have happened that couldn't have waited for the morrow."

She sighed, exasperated with his stubborn refusal to acknowledge the obvious. "I believe you know precisely why I am here." When he said nothing, she asked, "Are you courting Rose Hardwick?"

He looked pointedly at the clock again before answering, but she recognized the action for the delaying tactic that it was.

"Surely you're not here at this hour to satisfy your curiosity about the latest on-dit."

"You didn't answer the question."

His eyes narrowed. "Lady Worthington is a close personal friend to my mother. It is not an acquaintance I can avoid."

She wanted to shake him. "What does that mean? That you're merely being friendly? That there's an understanding between your two families about you and Rose?"

He shook his head. "No, there is no such understanding. Regardless of what the Worthingtons choose to believe."

"Do you want there to be one?" She forced the question out, not sure she wanted to know the answer anymore.

He was silent a moment before he answered. "No. I do not."

Hope threatened to steal her breath. "Because you care for me." She ignored him when he shook his head again. "You kissed me that night at Almack's. Why would you do that if you didn't care for me even a little?"

He couldn't meet her eyes. "If you'll wait here, I'll arrange for a carriage to take you home."

She believed him when he said that he didn't wish to be with Rose Hardwick, but it was clear he was still resisting their own connection. She'd felt the evidence of his desire for her that evening at Almack's when he'd kissed her. Beyond that, he wasn't the type of man to lead her astray. If he didn't care for her, he would have no difficulty telling her so.

Something was holding him back, but she suffered from no such qualms. What remained was to show him how she felt.

She untied the ribbon holding her cloak closed and turned to drape the garment over a chair. When she faced him again, she didn't miss the fact that his eyes had been trained on her figure. The pale green gown she wore was modest, and for a moment she wished she'd changed into one of her evening dresses with a lower décolletage. Kerrick didn't seem to mind, and the appreciation in his gaze gave her the courage to speak.

"I'm not returning home. Not yet. Perhaps later, after we've…" She let her voice trail off, not quite brave enough to say the words, but from his expression it was clear she didn't need to.

When he replied, his voice was filled with regret. "This isn't going to happen, Catherine. It can't."

She took another step forward, her spirits rising when he didn't back away from her. "I think we both know that isn't true."

His eyes searched her face and she could see that he was very close, finally, to accepting what had always been inevitable.

"I'm supposed to keep you safe, not ruin you."

She shook her head and took the final step that removed the distance between them. They were so close now she could feel the heat of his body reaching out to her. Beckoning to her. "I don't care about that. I only care about being with you."

In an attempt to keep some distance between them, he raised his hands to her arms. The heat of his fingers on her bare skin had an almost dizzying effect on her.

"You should care, Catherine. I want…" A spasm of

emotion crossed his face. "You know what I want, but until I am free, I am in no position to make promises."

"I am not asking you to make promises."

His eyes squeezed closed as though he were in pain. "We can't do this."

Instead of gripping her arms tightly to keep her away, his fingers relaxed and his thumbs made little circles on her skin where he held her just above her elbows. Despite his words to the contrary, his resolve was weakening. She moved closer to him. He resisted for only a moment, and then his grip slackened. Taking advantage of his moment of weakness, she raised her arms to clasp his shoulders and pressed herself against his hard chest, rejoicing when his breath shuddered.

"Kerrick."

He must have heard her need, because his eyes snapped open. Heat blazed in their depths, almost searing her with their intensity.

"I want this," she said.

"You don't know what you're asking."

"I know exactly what I'm asking. I also know that whatever happens, I will have no regrets, even if we can only have this one night together."

This time there was no hesitation when he released her arms and drew her more firmly against him. He lowered his head and took her mouth with a desperation that threatened to steal her breath. A corresponding need rose swiftly within her.

She was actually going to make love to the man she couldn't imagine being without. She'd told him she didn't need the promise of a future together to be with him tonight, and she'd meant those words. That didn't mean she'd stop hoping for more. But for now, this would be enough.

Her tongue warred with his as she wove her fingers into his hair. She was afraid to let go lest this turn out to be only a dream. When he pulled back, she started to protest.

"Shhh." He laid a finger over her lips to forestall her argument.

Mere inches separated them, and she could still feel the warmth of his breath on her face. Acting purely on instinct, she clasped his hand between hers and drew his finger into her mouth, circling it with her tongue and drawing on it. His eyes darkened with approval.

"You're the very devil," he said, removing his finger and running it over her now-sensitized mouth. "A temptress sent to lead me into the flames of hell. But it would take more strength than I possess to stop now. You do not, however, deserve to be deflowered on the floor of my study."

He took her hand again, this time leading her down

the darkened corridor to the main stairs. She was relieved when they reached his bedroom without encountering any of the household staff. It had taken all her nerve tonight to come, alone, to his home, and she didn't think she had any bravery left for knowing glances and whispered words belowstairs.

His bedroom was a reflection of him. Dark, masculine. What surprised her most, however, was the lavender orchid in a small vase on his night table. Was that a coincidence, or had he remembered her telling Mr. Clifton how much she loved orchids?

He must have noticed the direction of her glance for he cleared his throat before saying, "I've always appreciated beauty."

His eyes were not on the flower, however, but on her. The compliment warmed her right down to her toes and chased away the last of her inhibitions. She turned to face him and placed a hand directly over his heart where she could feel its steady beat.

She licked her lips before saying, "You must show me what to do."

He mirrored her action, placing his hand first over her upper chest before moving it lower. Instead of settling over her heart, however, he cupped one of her breasts in his large hand. She sucked in a breath, only to release it again with a surprised puff of air when his thumb moved over its peak. His other hand rose to do the same to her other breast, and pleasure speared through her.

"To begin," he said, his voice more rough than she had ever remembered, "we are wearing far too much clothing."

He spun her around and made quick work of the ties of her dress and the strings of her stays, his familiarity with women's clothing further proof that he was much more experienced than she. Before stripping the clothing from her body, he took the time to remove the pins from her hair and spread his fingers through the heavy mass. She closed her eyes in bliss when he nuzzled her ear.

When he drew her dress away from her body, allowing it to fall at her feet with a whisper of satin, and cast aside her corset, she was glad that she was facing away from him. Still wearing her chemise, she leaned back into him, craving his touch, and he complied by bringing his hands around and cupping her breasts yet again. He lowered his head to the side of her throat, and she shivered when his mouth settled on her skin.

She tilted her head to the side to grant him further access.

"Catherine, you undo me," he said, his breath warm against her skin.

She very much doubted he could feel more cast adrift than she at that moment. His hands moved to the neckline of her chemise, and when she realized that he planned to remove it, she covered his hands with hers to still his movement. She turned in his arms.

"I am not the only one wearing too much clothing," she said, aiming for a levity she was far from feeling.

He took a step back and she could almost feel the caress of his eyes on her as his gaze roamed over her body.

"I would never wish to disappoint you."

He made quick work of his cravat and the buttons of his waistcoat, and when he was done, Catherine stepped forward to draw his tailcoat from his shoulders. Mirroring his casual disregard for her own clothing, she dropped the garment to the floor before doing the same with his waistcoat.

"You are a quick student," he said, an edge to his voice.

"I aim only to please," she replied as she pulled his shirt from his trousers and burrowed her hands underneath the material so she could finally feel his skin.

Remembering how it had felt when he'd teased her breasts, she trailed her fingers up his torso, dragging the lawn fabric of his shirt upward as she sought his nipples. She raked her nails over them gently and was rewarded by his harsh inhalation.

He stripped his shirt over his head in one quick movement and threw it onto the floor. Without further preamble, he dragged down her chemise until her breasts were freed and then lowered his head to take one aching peak into his mouth. All thought deserted her. Afraid her knees would buckle at any moment, she could only cling to his shoulders as he suckled her. One hand toyed with her other breast while the other hand cupped her backside and shifted the lower half of her body until she was held firmly against him. His arousal pressed into her, but not where she ached for him between her legs, and she squirmed against him.

He gripped her chemise where it rested at her waist, and she felt the first flare of alarm when he knelt before her. Her hands fluttered to his shoulders in uncertainty.

"What are you doing?" She could not keep the quaver from her voice.

He looked up at her, his normally vivid blue eyes now almost black. "I'm trying to make sure you enjoy this as much as I know I will."

"Kerrick, I—"

But he ignored her protest and released his hold on her chemise. It pooled at her feet, and she stood before him in only her shoes and stockings. He made a low sound of approval before kissing her belly. She was still slightly alarmed by what he was doing, but that feeling turned to outright shock when he parted her legs and blew softly on her now-damp curls.

Her legs started to buckle and he rose swiftly when she swayed forward. Before she knew what he was doing, he'd lifted her into his arms, carried her to his large bed, and deposited her onto it. She knew enough about what happened between a man and a woman to expect him to remove his trousers and join her on the bed. Instead, he drew her legs apart and devoured her with his eyes.

Embarrassed, she flung an arm over her eyes. She wouldn't stop him, not now, but her bravery threatened to desert her at the almost unbearable intimacy of being laid open to his hungry gaze.

Nothing happened for several moments.

"Catherine?"

This was Kerrick, the man she loved. She did not need to feel shy about him seeing her like this.

She lifted her arm and looked at him where he stood between her open thighs, uncertainty etched on his face. His concern only served to make her feel young and foolish. Fearing she'd disappointed him and needing to get away from his unrelenting gaze, she rolled over onto her stomach and closed her eyes.

The bed shifted under his weight as he lowered himself onto the bed beside her. His warm hand settled on the bare skin of her lower back, and when he spoke his voice was strained.

"I'll understand if you've reconsidered. I won't be particularly pleased about it, but we can stop right now. You haven't been fully compromised yet—"

Needing him to stop talking, she surprised them both by turning and launching herself at him. He rolled onto his back and she settled over him, her slight frame supported by his much larger one.

She made a soft sound in the back of her throat as she delighted in the feel of his skin against hers. She was aware of many sensations all at once: his heat seeping into her, her breasts crushed against his muscled chest, the sprinkling of hair abrading her nipples. He still wore his trousers, but there was no mistaking the hard ridge of his erection pressing into her thigh. And his scent... why had she never noticed how wonderful he smelled before now? She was almost light-headed from the onslaught of sensation.

"You haven't reconsidered, then."

She shook her head and then there were no more words. He clasped her head in his hands, his fingers tangling in the mass of her hair. Their eyes met and held for several long seconds.

Her breath shuddered when he urged her head down and claimed her mouth with a soul-stirring kiss. Her world constricted until there was only Kerrick and only this moment between them. He let her take the lead in the kiss, and she explored his mouth, her tongue warring with his with an intensity that almost frightened her. Dimly, she became aware of his hands sweeping a trail of fire down her back before settling on her hips. He shifted her until her legs draped on either side of his hips, and she moaned at the feel of his hard length pressed right where she needed him most.

He broke the kiss then and spoke, his lips still on hers. "Do you trust me?"

She did. With her very life. She nodded and he rolled them both over until she lay beneath him, his weight braced over her. Thinking that he meant to take her in that moment, she wrapped her arms around his shoulders and tried to draw him even closer.

"Not yet, my impatient one."

She made a sound of protest when he levered himself off her, but he ignored her and started trailing kisses down her body. Her objections ceased when he stopped to lavish attention on her breasts. He suckled each one in turn, each pull from his mouth causing an almost desperate ache much lower, even though he no longer pressed against her.

"This is too much," she said, the pleasure almost overwhelming.

He lifted his head and his eyes locked with hers, a wicked gleam in their depths. "We have barely begun." His words, coupled with the intensity of his gaze, promised unimaginable pleasure, and she shivered in response.

He pressed an openmouthed kiss low on her belly, then shifted lower still. This time she pushed aside her alarm when he kissed the inside of her thigh, unwilling to let her nerves put an end to their lovemaking. For that's what this was. She loved him and she needed him.

Some instinct told her what he wanted, and she parted her thighs for him. He made a sound that could only be described as an approving growl before touching her where no one ever had.

"You're already wet for me," he said, stroking her.

"I never imagined such things."

She wasn't sure if she'd spoken the words aloud, and in the next moment she didn't care. He moved his hand, replacing it with his tongue. The shocking sensation, coupled with the warmth of his breath where she had never expected to feel it, had her squirming.

"Kerrick...," she breathed.

She was close to losing her mind, but he didn't stop. His tongue drew circles on a particularly sensitive spot, and he thrust first one, then two fingers inside her. As he continued to torment her, both inside and out, she quickly spiraled out of control until her body seemed to fly apart.

She might have screamed—she honestly couldn't say—as tremors wracked her body. He didn't stop, prolonging the torment, until the last quiver passed.

She was incapable of movement and could only lay still, every muscle in her body languid, as he moved to cover her again. When he kissed her, she could taste herself on his lips. He pressed the tip of his erection against her entrance, and her body stirred to life again, wanting this final, ultimate act of intimacy.

She was so wet, so ready and aching for him, that the first stab of pain at his penetration took her by surprise. He stilled at her sharp cry, pressing. He rested his forehead against hers, and they remained that way for what must have been a full minute, their breaths mingling together.

"You're so tight. Tell me I can move now before I lose my mind completely."

She replied by contracting her muscles, squeezing him when he rested inside her, and he groaned. He started to draw himself out and she panicked, thinking he meant to pull out of her completely and knowing that he hadn't yet found his own completion. When he pushed himself back in, more slowly this time, her body gave only a slight twinge. His next penetration hurt even less, and then she was meeting him thrust for thrust, all memory of pain forgotten.

"I can't..." He started to move faster and his urgency called out to her, quickening her pleasure until she peaked a second time. He pushed himself inside her one final time before cursing and pulling out of her completely. He groaned and spilled himself outside her body.

It took her a few seconds to realize what had happened. He'd pulled out to prevent her from conceiving a child. Her mind knew it was the right thing to do—the only way he could protect her. Her emotions, however, could latch on to only one thought.

No promises, he'd said. She and Kerrick might never marry, never have a life together. Never have children.

A wave of sadness passed over her, and not wanting him to see it, she turned her head when he lifted himself from her and drew her back into his arms. They lay like that for several minutes, her head pillowed on his chest, his arms wrapped around her as their breathing slowed and the sweat from their bodies cooled. Her head rested over his heart, her hand at his waist. Neither spoke, knowing that to do so would put an end to their brief interlude together.

Despair threatened to consume her when she realized she'd made a terrible mistake. Not in coming there—she could never regret what they had shared. She'd expected that this one night of stolen passion would bring only happiness. A memory for her to hoard away and look back upon with something akin to fondness. At the very least, she'd thought it would give her joy to know she'd reached out and grasped a chance to share the ultimate intimacy with the man she loved.

She'd been very naive in her certainty of how she'd feel afterward. She realized that it would now be so much worse, knowing what she and Kerrick might have had together.

She was certain that if he was free to do so, he'd choose her over Rose Hardwick. But there was something linking him to that family, and she had no way of knowing if he would ever be free.

In the silence that surrounded them, she became aware that his heartbeat had begun to speed up again. She lifted her head to look at him, expecting to see desire in his eyes. What she saw, instead, drove away the saucy comment she'd been about to make.

"Kerrick?"

"You were correct to suspect I was hiding something from you."

CHAPTER SEVEN

His decision made, Kerrick didn't want to waste any more time pushing Catherine away. Brantford would have his hide if he even suspected he was about to confide in her, but Kerrick knew that the woman in his arms could be trusted to keep his secrets. He wouldn't make the same mistake Nicholas had made with Louisa the previous fall when he'd done everything in his power to push her away. It meant he was a selfish bastard, but Kerrick wanted to give her a reason to wait for him. The question, though, was whether she would be able to stand back and watch him continue to pay court to another woman.

She sat up and his eyes moved straight to her breasts. Desire began to stir again, and he cursed softly. He stood and retrieved his dressing gown.

"I'm not sure I'll be able to keep my thoughts on the subject at hand with you sitting there looking ripe for the plucking."

The corners of her mouth lifted in that special smile she used when she thought he was being amusing and a little ridiculous, but she did take the dressing gown and rose to stand. He watched while she swung the garment around her shoulders, his hands itching to reach out for her again. Only when she was covered did he tear his eyes away and reach for his trousers.

When he looked at her again, she was sitting cross-legged in the middle of his bed, her fair hair tumbling down her back. She looked at once very young and very desirable. He lowered himself onto the edge of the bed beside her and ran a hand over his face.

He glanced up when she shifted closer and placed a hand on his knee.

"I know about your work."

He'd been wrestling with just how much to confide in her, and her statement caught him off guard. He kept his voice neutral when he asked, "My work?"

She nodded. "Yes. I know you're a spy."

He gaped at her for a moment before collecting

himself. "Why would you say that?"

"Louisa told me."

He winced. "Your sister told you I was a spy? Why would she think that?"

She waved her hand in dismissal, as if she were stating something as obvious as the color of the sun. "Overlea suspects you have dealings with the Home Office, and you're always disappearing. And tonight at the Worthingtons' musicale you disappeared for some time and didn't want anyone to know."

He'd been so certain no one had seen him slip out of the room that her revelation shook him. He gripped her hand. "Did anyone else see me?"

She shook her head and he released his breath, relief flooding through him.

"I wanted you to think I was enjoying the music, but in truth I was too busy watching you."

Light color stained her cheeks at the admission. He followed the blush down her throat and was distracted, wondering just how far down her skin the color traveled. It was with great difficulty that he brought himself back to the subject at hand.

"I'm not a spy." At her expression of disbelief, he continued, "I've helped out here and there gathering information, but that is all."

She tilted her head to the side, a slight crease

marking her forehead. "Is that not what a spy does?"

Perhaps she did have a point. "I suppose you're right. I've been comparing my actions to some of the more dangerous endeavors of others in the government's employ..." He covered her mouth with his fingers, his tone one of exaggerated patience when he said, "And no, I will not tell you about whom I speak."

She drew his hand away and crossed her arms. "I could guess—in fact I think I already know who else is involved—but I'll leave that for another time."

He'd have to worry about that later. "At any rate, I can't reveal the nature of my mission, but I want you to know that I am doing all within my power to find the answers to the matter I've been asked to look into. Once that is done, my spying, as you call it, will be over."

She was quiet for several long moments. "I can help you," she said when she finally spoke again.

Dread curled in his belly at the innocent excitement in her voice. "No, Catherine. This isn't a game."

"It's Lord Worthington, is it not? You're trying to gather information about him. Is that why you're courting Rose?"

He shook his head, but she pressed on.

"I can befriend Rose. We're of an age and I know

she doesn't dislike me."

"Absolutely not—" He came to an abrupt halt when he realized his vehement response had just confirmed her guess.

"Of course I can," she said, her smile one he would expect to see an adult use with a small child. "I'm not foolish enough to come right out and ask her about whether her father is engaged in any suspicious activity. What could be more normal than one young woman calling on another and forming a friendship? No one would think anything of it, and it will allow me, from time to time, to call upon her. I might even see if Lord Worthington is receiving any suspicious guests."

His frustration—and fear—mounted in the face of her insistence on injecting herself into his investigation. He closed his eyes and counted to ten before opening them again and replying. "It is highly unlikely that anyone engaged in any type of illegal activity would receive calls from their accomplices during official calling hours. And no, this is not an admission that I am investigating Worthington."

"In that case, you have no cause at all to worry if I call on Rose tomorrow afternoon."

He wanted to say something more, but Catherine, clever girl that she was proving herself to be, distracted him by undoing the belt of the dressing gown and shrugging out of the garment. He conceded defeat for the moment and pushed her onto her back. He would argue with her later, when he could think again.

CATHERINE ARRIVED HOME shortly before dawn and was able to sneak up to her room without being seen. She'd gotten very little sleep while with Kerrick and, not wanting to arouse her family's suspicions, didn't sleep past her usual time that morning. But her lack of sleep didn't affect her mood. Energy seemed to surge within her, and she was finding it difficult to keep a perpetual smile from her face. She didn't even bother when she was alone, but she made the effort to school her expression when others were present.

Now, standing before the Worthingtons' town house that afternoon, her maid Lily by her side, she lifted the heavy knocker and let it fall with a determined thump. The door was opened moments later by a stately butler who accepted her card and showed her into the drawing room. There she found Rose Hardwick seated on a low chaise longue. She wasn't surprised to find her surrounded by her usual court of admirers.

Her dark hair styled no less elaborately than she normally wore it for evening entertainments, the voluptuous brunette looked radiant in a demure dress of white with pale blue ribbons that accented the neckline and hem. Catherine was glad she'd made sure to look her best. She still felt like a pale shadow beside the more vivacious beauty of the other woman, but the night she'd spent with Kerrick had gone a long way toward making her realize that he felt no real animosity for the woman before her now.

If Rose was surprised to see her, she didn't show it when she looked away from a young man who was in the process of trying to cajole her to go for a drive in the park. In fact, she was the one surprised when Rose stood and crossed the room to clasp Catherine's hands between her own.

"I'm so glad you're finally here," Rose said.

Catherine was confused by the enthusiastic greeting, but that confusion cleared when Rose turned back to face the six men who'd all risen when she stood.

"I'm afraid I've made other plans with Miss Evans for the rest of the afternoon," she said, a mischievous twinkle in her eyes as her gaze met Catherine's. "I'll have to say my good-byes now, but I'm sure to see some of you later this evening."

Catherine almost laughed aloud at the identical expressions of disappointment on the men's faces.

"Where will you be?" one of them called out after them, but Rose had already linked her arm through

Catherine's and turned her around.

"Don't slow down or look back," Rose murmured under her breath as she led them toward the back of the house. She didn't stop until they'd escaped into the back garden. After closing the door behind them, she dropped Catherine's arm and sank into one of several chairs that had been set out on the small terrace. "I'm sorry if I startled you."

Catherine took a seat next to her. She considered the best approach to take and settled finally on honesty. "I'll admit I'm surprised you felt the need to escape."

Rose aimed a direct look at her. "You think I'm frivolous and that I like being surrounded by those prancing fools."

It wasn't a question, and Catherine found herself apologizing. "Yes, I'm afraid so. You do present that appearance."

Rose sighed. "I know, and I don't blame you for believing that. It is, after all, what I want others to see."

Since they were being honest, Catherine didn't demur. "I do find it difficult to believe you don't enjoy the attention."

Rose smiled. "I admit it's not all an act. I do enjoy seeing just how far some of them will go to capture my interest. You would not credit some of the gifts I've received."

"But your interest lies elsewhere."

"Yes," Rose said, looking away.

Catherine didn't want to ask the next question, especially not after what had happened the night before, but she had to know.

"Lord Kerrick?"

Rose didn't reply right away, and Catherine felt her spirits sink. It was true then. Rose really had missed Kerrick when he'd been away from town, and she really did want to marry him. It must be killing her that he spent so much time with Catherine's family. She wondered if the other woman suspected Kerrick's interest lay not only in interacting with his friend of many years, but with that friend's new sister-in-law. With her.

Rose's reply was so low Catherine almost didn't hear it. "No."

"No?" Her mind reeled and she almost cried out with relief. Instead, she took a few moments to compose herself before asking, "But your parents expect there to be a match between you. And you've just admitted you don't care for the young men who were here today."

"Oh, the man in question has no clue I'm even alive."

The laugh she gave was a bitter one, and Catherine

realized then why Rose acted the way she did.

"You're trying to capture his attention, this man who doesn't seem to see you."

Rose's mouth turned up at the corners in a ghost of a smile. "I'm so very glad you came here today. I suspected I'd like you but didn't know if you'd welcome my overtures of friendship." She hesitated a moment before adding, "Especially not since you're in love with Lord Kerrick and all of society has the two of us practically married."

Catherine was alarmed at the other woman's insight. "Good lord, am I that obvious?" She closed her eyes as horror swept through her. She wondered how she could possibly face Rose's parents if they were home.

Rose reached forward and laid a hand over hers, squeezing it lightly before letting go. "Not to everyone. I daresay my parents and others think it's just a casual acquaintance. It's well known that Kerrick is good friends with Lord Overlea, and you are his wife's sister."

"But you saw right through that."

Rose shrugged. "I am going through the same thing myself. It wasn't difficult to see that same emotion reflected in you. I've seen the way you look at him, especially when he dances with me. It wasn't difficult to figure out why that would be."

Catherine licked her lips, hesitating briefly before asking the question that lay unspoken between them. "I'm afraid I haven't been as astute as you. Who is it you care for?"

Rose leaned back in her chair, making no attempt to hide her pain. "That's because he doesn't attend the usual evening entertainments, and when he does, he doesn't dance. Not with me and rarely with anyone else." She laughed, clearly seeing that Catherine was trying to sift through all the men she'd met during her time in London.

"I'm sorry for prying," Catherine said.

Rose considered her closely. "We don't know one another, but I have a very good feeling about you. If there were even the slightest chance... Well, there's no point in discussing something that will never happen."

Catherine's heart ached at the look of hopelessness on Rose's face. Given how well the past day had gone for her, she wished she could help the woman the whole *ton* saw as Kerrick's all-but-in-name fiancée. This was such a different side to the Rose Hardwick everyone had seen since the season began, and she was no less than stunned by the revelation. She was also very glad that she'd chosen to call that afternoon. She had a feeling the two of them could be great friends.

"If you ever change your mind and decide you want to talk to someone, I'll be there for you. I'm afraid I've never tried my hand at matchmaking, but maybe between the two of us we could come up with some way to capture this man's interest."

The smile that Rose gave her was a hollow one. "With any luck, I might take you up on your offer. But until that day…" She stood, her brave mask back in place, and swept a hand over the overgrown garden. "I've heard that you're very knowledgeable about plants. Our gardener fell ill recently and hasn't been able to tend to the garden properly. To be honest, I've never been particularly fond of it. Too ordinary. What say you we take inventory and come up with a new layout to present to my parents?"

Catherine's critical eye moved over the simple landscape before returning to settle on Rose. "Simple or elaborate?"

"Oh, elaborate, of course. The more flamboyant, the better."

Somehow Catherine kept from leaping up and hugging the other woman. An entire garden to plan? Given what she'd seen during her visit to Kew Gardens, her mind was already brimming with ideas for plants to introduce and possible configurations. It would also give her reason to visit the Worthingtons' town house often and perhaps learn something that would help Kerrick.

"This is going to be great fun," she said, standing and following Rose down the two steps of the terrace and into the garden proper.

CHAPTER EIGHT

When she returned after her visit with Rose, Catherine was surprised to learn that Kerrick was visiting. He hadn't said anything about it when they'd parted early that morning.

She entered the drawing room a little too quickly, heart racing at the knowledge she'd be seeing him again so soon, but was disappointed to find only her sister there. Louisa was working on a needlepoint pattern she planned to turn into a decorative pillow for the nursery. Louisa looked up at her entrance and sighed with barely contained exasperation.

"Kerrick is in the study with Nicholas. He's staying

for supper tonight before we go to the theater."

Catherine sat on the settee beside her sister and looked down at the needlework on Louisa's lap. Only a small corner of the pattern was completed. "What did you finally settle on?" she asked.

"A lamb."

Catherine frowned. "A black one?"

Louisa shrugged, a wry smile playing about her lips. "Given Nicholas's reputation before he settled down, I figured it was a fun idea. And I know you're trying to change the subject."

"There was a subject? I only just arrived."

Louisa peered at her closely, and it was all Catherine could do not to look away in embarrassment.

"You're in a good mood today," she said finally. "Who did you visit this afternoon?"

"Rose Hardwick," Catherine said, knowing that was the last name her sister expected to hear.

Louisa raised a brow. "Care to tell me why?"

Catherine shrugged. "We're of an age and she seems nice." She hesitated before adding, "It turns out she was glad for the diversion. It would appear she doesn't have many friends."

"Perhaps not female friends, but half the men of the *ton* would love to be much more."

Catherine found herself feeling defensive on Rose's

behalf. "I quite like her."

Startled by her vehemence, Louisa said, "I didn't mean offense."

Catherine sank back against the settee and took a deep breath to steady her nerves. She wasn't used to keeping things from her sister, and now she found herself keeping all sorts of secrets. She also had to admit that she felt a small stab of shame for her behavior the previous night. She knew now that Rose's affections were engaged elsewhere, but that hadn't been the case the previous night. In pursuing Kerrick, she hadn't even considered whether she was hurting the other woman. She'd cared only about herself and what she wanted. It was an eye-opening experience to realize she could be capable of such selfishness.

"Rose would like me to plan a new garden for their town house. She hopes to present it to her parents once I've come up with and drawn a design."

Louisa was silent for a moment before saying, "Won't that complicate things? I thought she'd be the last person you'd want to befriend. Especially given the understanding that seems to be between Kerrick and her family."

Catherine looked away, knowing she could betray the confidences of neither Kerrick nor Rose. Kerrick seemed to think it was vital for his inquiries that people continue to believe he was hoping to marry Rose. She picked up the needlework her sister had cast aside and traced a finger along the stitches in what she hoped was a casual movement.

"I can be friends with both of them."

Louisa was silent for almost a full minute. Catherine looked up finally, careful to keep her expression neutral. The confusion and concern on her older sister's face made her feel a twinge of guilt.

"Everything is well, Louisa. Trust me."

Her sister sighed. "I'm trying to, but I don't want to see you hurt if things turn out as everyone seems to believe they will."

"I'm all grown up now. You can't shelter me forever."

Louisa leaned sideways and bumped a shoulder against hers. "Old habits die hard."

They were laughing when Kerrick entered the room and Catherine had to glance away. After what they had shared the previous night, she was aware of him in a way she'd never been before. Somehow she was going to have to keep others from suspecting that anything had happened between them, and she wasn't sure if she'd be able to accomplish that feat.

When she did look back, she managed a small smile that was a pale shadow of the one she wished to give him. His expression was carefully neutral as he returned her greeting. He turned to listen to something her sister was saying, and Catherine felt a painful flash of doubt. Had the previous night meant as much to him as it had to her? She knew he'd had paramours before her, and for a moment she wondered if she was just another in a long line of women.

She pushed back the depressing thought. She'd never been one to dwell on the negative and she wouldn't begin now. Kerrick wasn't free to reveal his feelings for her, but she knew he cared for her. She would have to hold on to that belief.

Kerrick turned his attention to Louisa. "Your husband has requested your presence in the study. I think he just received a number of bills from the dressmaker."

Louisa rolled her eyes and stood. "I can't imagine why he's surprised. There are two of us, and I've seen some of his bills from the tailor."

Catherine remained seated. She wanted—no, needed—to speak to Kerrick. Louisa arched a brow as she looked down at her and Catherine returned a sunny smile. Her sister was shaking her head as she departed the room, leaving her alone with Kerrick.

When Louisa was gone, Kerrick turned his attention back to Catherine. She hoped he would sit next to her on the settee, but he lowered himself into the same chair again. Now that they were alone, Catherine was free to drink in his appearance. Relief coursed through her when he dropped the polite mask he'd been wearing and gazed at her with the same longing she felt.

"How are you feeling today?" he asked.

She knew he was asking about physical pain, but waved a hand in dismissal. "Fine. Happy."

"You don't appear happy."

She exhaled a frustrated sigh. "It is more difficult than I imagined, seeing you again and having to pretend there is nothing between us." She paused for a moment, considering whether she should admit her worries. In the end, she merely hinted at her primary concern. She didn't think she'd ever be ready to learn how he really felt about Louisa.

"But that isn't all that's troubling you."

She shook her head. "You are very good at keeping your feelings hidden. I feared last night meant no more to you than any other night…" Unable to finish the thought, she let her voice trail off.

"Than any other night I've spent with a woman."

She felt heat creep into her face and had to look away. She was surprised when he moved to sit next to her and reached for her hands.

"Look at me, Catherine."

She didn't want to, but he cupped her cheek and turned her face to him. His thumb stroked her lower lip, and she didn't miss the way his eyes darkened slightly before he dropped his hand. He still held one of her hands in his.

"Last night was like no other night I've experienced. You affect me like no other woman has before. You know I'm not in a position right now to offer for you, but I would if I didn't have this damned investigation to look into."

Her heart had started to race when he first touched her, and when he mentioned offering for her it actually seemed to skip a beat. He hadn't said he loved her, but she'd always been a good judge of character and she could tell now he wasn't lying. He did care for her. Still, she couldn't help prodding.

"You're saying…"

"I'm asking you to be patient with me."

The corner of Kerrick's mouth quirked up in amusement when she answered his plea with an exaggerated sigh. She was frustrated when he dropped her hand and shifted away from her on the settee, but she understood why he needed to place distance between them. Given that a servant, or Heaven forbid Louisa or Nicholas, could walk in at any moment, she really couldn't blame him. The door to the room stood open and she had no way of telling if anyone had already seen them.

"I called on Rose this afternoon," she said.

His eyes narrowed. "I asked you not to."

"I quite like her. She and I are embarking on a project together. A gardening project," she was quick to add when she saw his obvious concern. "I'll be safe. Unless, of course, you fear Rose is also involved in whatever it is you are investigating?"

He merely shook his head in exasperation. "I doubt very much that Rose Hardwick has it in her to be capable of any duplicity."

"You might be surprised about that." At his open disbelief, she added, "She has hidden depths."

"Really?"

She gave him a look of mock reprimand. "You are forbidden from considering her hidden depths."

He was laughing when Louisa returned to tell her it was time to dress for dinner and their evening out.

IT TOOK ALL his acting ability to survive the meal. Seated opposite Catherine, Kerrick found it almost impossible it keep from devouring her with his eyes. She clearly had no idea how she affected him if she thought it was easy for him to appear oblivious to her charms.

He suspected she'd dressed in such a way as to ensure he'd have a difficult time keeping up that pretense. The low-cut bodice of her gown was well within the bounds of propriety, but that didn't mean he hadn't been surprised when he'd first set eyes on her in the pale yellow gown. Against her fair hair, the color made her appear to glow, and her breasts were offered up like treats to be devoured. He'd seen her smile of satisfaction at his shock when she came down for dinner. He'd wanted nothing more in that moment than to whisk her off to a quiet corner of the house where no one would find them, strip that gown from her, and uncover the delights he knew lay beneath.

When he'd turned to greet Louisa, he'd noticed her frown and responded with a small shrug of helplessness. He was only a mortal man, after all. How did she expect him to react when presented with such a feast for the eyes? Fortunately, Nicholas hadn't seen his reaction. He counted himself lucky his friend was so preoccupied with worry for his wife's delicate condition that he had eyes for no one but her. If Nicholas learned about what had passed between him and Catherine the night before... His mind skittered away from completing that thought. They might be the best of friends, but he wouldn't be surprised if his friend called him out over the matter.

They made their way to the theater in the Overlea carriage. He hadn't thought to ask what play was showing since the *ton* generally went to the theater not for the entertainment but to be seen by others. If the play being shown was an enjoyable one, that was merely a side benefit. He almost laughed aloud when he saw the playbill.

The Taming of the Shrew.

How appropriate that the shrew in question was named Katherine, Kerrick thought. Not that Catherine was shrewish, but she could certainly do with some taming. The last thing he needed was to worry about her unintentionally putting herself in harm's way. He knew she was likely correct in her assumption that there was little danger in befriending Rose Hardwick. Still, he wanted her as far removed from the Worthingtons, and even the faintest possibility of danger, as possible. He didn't think Worthington was a violent man, but the same might not be true about the others with whom he was involved.

He doubted very much that he could convince the Overleas to take Catherine far away from London. Not without explaining the reason for his concern. It was vital that no one suspect his interest in the Worthingtons lay with the father and not the daughter. His actions over the past day had already jeopardized his mission.

Louisa and Catherine had just relinquished their wraps to the waiting attendants when Miss Hardwick approached them. He hoped Worthington wouldn't be far, but when he looked beyond her he saw, instead, the ever-present coterie of young men who seemed to follow her everywhere she went.

He was surprised to see what appeared to be genuine affection between the two young women when they greeted one another, and he wondered what miracle Catherine had wrought to make that happen.

What almost jostled him out of his equanimity, however, was the flirtatious glance Rose aimed his way as he took her hand and bowed over it. This was new. Rose normally appeared to barely tolerate his company. Just what *had* gone on between the two women that afternoon?

After they'd exchanged a few pleasantries about the weather, Rose asked for permission to whisk Catherine away. He became alarmed when the girl started to lead Catherine to the group of young men waiting for her return.

"Miss Hardwick," he called out after them.

Rose turned to face him. "Yes, my lord?"

He wanted to tell her to leave Catherine alone. To keep her away from the wolves who would descend upon her if given even the slightest encouragement, which so far this season she hadn't seemed to offer. What he said, instead, was, "Are you here with your parents tonight?"

He ignored the frown both Louisa and Nicholas aimed at him. The only thing that mattered was that Catherine knew he was putting on a show of courting the Worthingtons' favor.

Rose glanced at Catherine before replying. "They've gone ahead to our box. Mother has a touch of the headache and wasn't up for the noise of the crowds."

"That sounds like a great idea," Louisa said, smiling up at her husband. "I feel a little tired this evening as well."

If Nicholas could have carried her the rest of the way, Kerrick had a very strong suspicion he would have done so. His wife wouldn't have been pleased at the extra attention such an action would have earned them, though. After exacting his promise to show Catherine up to their box, Nicholas and Louisa left him.

It was still twenty-five minutes before the performance was due to begin. Kerrick made the rounds, greeting acquaintances along the way and stopping not far from where he'd started only a few minutes later. He'd been trying to appear unconcerned that his would-be fiancée and the woman he really wanted were both surrounded by young bucks eager to impress. The first was easy to accomplish, but the second was decidedly more difficult. He heard Catherine laugh at something one of the men said, and he knew the scowl that momentarily appeared before he could smooth it over would be seen as yet another indication of his intentions toward Miss Hardwick.

"She's lovely, isn't she?" Lord Standish had come to a stop beside him and was staring with almost eager interest at Catherine and Rose.

He hoped Standish was referring to Rose, but his next words told him otherwise.

"It's a pity you're promised to the other one. But your loss is my gain."

Kerrick's blood turned to ice and he turned to face Standish. Despite the fact that he managed to keep from baring his teeth, no one would miss the threat implicit in his words. "You would do well to set your sights elsewhere."

Standish made a soft tsking sound. "Don't you think you're being greedy?" His gaze turned again to Catherine and there was no mistaking the lasciviousness in his expression. "Rest assured, Miss Evans will be mine."

When he turned to leave, Kerrick let him go without another word. Standish was known to thrive on conflict, and he'd be damned before he gave him the satisfaction of seeing that his words had struck terror in his heart.

He knew Nicholas would never allow Standish anywhere near Catherine. Still, he had to wrestle back the urge to march over to the group of young people—all of whom made him feel much older than this twenty-nine years—and drag Catherine away. Instead, he forced himself to make another circuit, even allowed himself to be dragged into conversation, before returning to collect Catherine.

She was smiling up at Lord Thornton, and the fact that he seemed to be amusing her soured his already dark mood.

"Your sister is no doubt wondering if you've gotten lost on the way to your seat."

"I'd be more than happy to escort you to Overlea's box," Thornton said, not bothering to hide his enthusiasm.

Kerrick was grinding his teeth together to stop from telling the man what he thought of his suggestion when Catherine turned to Thornton and smiled in apology. "They have already entrusted Lord Kerrick with the task," she said, taking the arm Kerrick offered.

Kerrick merely nodded to Rose and the men as he led Catherine away. They hadn't gone far when he said,

"You seemed to be enjoying yourself." His words came out sharper than he'd intended. If Catherine noticed his annoyance, she didn't show it.

"It was a little uncomfortable at first. I'm not used to being the center of attention. Back home there were very few young men my age, and what few there were certainly weren't interested in associating with a family that lived in near poverty. I'm just glad Rose was with me."

Normally he would have made some lighthearted, but nonetheless true, statement about what fools those boys had been. The fact that he didn't do so now went a long way toward showing just how annoyed Kerrick was with the way Catherine had seemed to revel in all the attention bestowed on her.

"You'll excuse me if I fail to thank her."

She looked up at him then, startled by his tone. "Is something the matter?"

He shook his head, annoyed at himself for what could only be seen as a gross overreaction on his part.

"You're angry."

Leave it to Catherine not to let the matter drop. "It is nothing."

A look of amazement lit her face. "It works," she breathed in wonder.

Her expression threw him completely off balance. It

reminded him so much of how she looked just before she came. He had to clear his throat before he could ask, "What works?"

"Her Grace… the Duchess of Clarington said that the best way to capture a man's attention was to show interest in another man. Or several other men."

He glared down at her. "Is that what you were doing? Trying to rouse my jealousy?" Never mind that it had worked.

She shook her head in denial. "Of course not. I have no reason to, do I? Not after last night."

"Catherine…," he said, voice low and sharp as he glanced around furtively to make sure no one had overheard.

She waved her hand in dismissal. "Don't worry. No one is near enough to hear."

She was going to be the death of him. Thankfully she said nothing further on the subject. They had reached the top of the stairs and started down the hallway outside the private boxes and there were people milling about.

He stopped short and had to pull Catherine to the side when someone almost ran into them. It took him a moment to realize it was Worthington. The older man seemed agitated and barely acknowledged them as he continued past. A prickle of unease settled at the base of Kerrick's skull and he turned in time to see another figure moving away quickly at the far end of the hall. He was too far away and Kerrick couldn't make out who it was. He could only see that it was a man with short brown hair and who seemed to be about his height. It could have been anyone. He considered following, but the man had melded into a group of theatergoers. Following him would only draw unwanted attention, and Kerrick couldn't be certain he'd be able to pinpoint him in the crowd.

"That was unusual," Catherine said, drawing Kerrick's thoughts back to her. "Lord Worthington never misses an opportunity to speak to you. I wonder what could have had him so preoccupied."

What, indeed. Damn. Perhaps Brantford's information was correct after all and Worthington had involved himself in something for which he was quite ill suited.

"He was probably anxious about not missing the beginning of the play." As if to underscore his words, the bells signaling that all guests should now be seated began to chime. "Come," he said, hoping to distract Catherine from the other man's curious behavior. "We should hurry before another search party is dispatched to find you."

KERRICK HAD TOO many things on his mind to pay attention to the play. Something or someone—the man he'd seen disappearing down the hallway?—had set Worthington on edge. He had only his instincts on which to base that suspicion, but he'd long since learned to ignore them at his own peril.

And then there was Catherine. She sat next to him and he longed to reach out to her. At the very least, he felt an almost overwhelming need to take one of her hands, which were clasped demurely on her lap, into his and just hold on to her. Assure himself that what had happened the night before had actually taken place and that the connection between them was real. But Louisa sat on the other side of Catherine, and there was no way she wouldn't see if he acted on his impulse. And so he sat there, trying to ignore both the urge to touch her and the scent of her that seemed to weave its way down to his very soul.

His frustration only mounted when Lord Thornton visited their box during the intermission. The frank appraisal on the other man's face when he noticed Catherine's low décolletage made him want to knock the boy's teeth into the back of his throat. Instead, he excused himself and made his way to Worthington's box.

As he'd expected, it was so filled with men vying for

Rose's attention that he barely had room to get inside. Upon seeing him, though, especially in the foul mood that had overtaken him, they stepped to the side to allow him passage.

He placed a light kiss on the back of Rose's gloved hand when she offered it to him, wondering briefly at the amusement in her eyes, and asked her if she was enjoying the performance.

"I always enjoy a good comedy, Lord Kerrick," she said, her manner telling him that she was referring to more than just the one taking place onstage.

"*Touché*, Miss Hardwick," he said, allowing his own amusement to show.

She inclined her head in acknowledgment of the compliment.

Damn, but Catherine was right. If he weren't forced to act the role of a man intent on making her his wife, he would actually like Rose Hardwick. Well, he didn't precisely dislike her now, but he wasn't altogether comfortable in her presence given the part he was playing.

Rose's attention was immediately captured by another young man when Kerrick turned to greet her parents.

"Lady Worthington, Lord Worthington," he said, taking a seat next to them. He couldn't help but notice how pale Lady Worthington looked, and he recalled Rose saying her mother was feeling unwell. The woman seated beside him now looked like she was suffering from more than just a headache. "I heard you weren't feeling quite yourself, Lady Worthington."

The smile she offered him was a pale imitation of her normally effusive one. "It is nothing that a good night's rest won't cure."

"And a few hours away from the constant crush, no doubt." There was no point in denying the crowds that surrounded the Worthingtons' daughter everywhere she went.

Lady Worthington shrugged, the small movement saying more effectively than words that she was used to it. No doubt she'd gone through the same when she was younger. Kerrick guessed she was only in her forties now, and she was still a striking woman. He wasn't sure how Worthington had managed to capture her as his wife, not if she'd been even half as popular as her daughter.

"I was thinking," he said, turning his attention now to her husband, "that we haven't yet had the opportunity to get to know one another very well. We should remedy that."

The carrot dangled, Worthington reached for it like a starving man. "That's a capital idea," he said, his chest puffing out as he contemplated the significance behind Kerrick's offer. He didn't come out and say it, but it was clear Worthington already thought of him as his all-but-in-name son-in-law. "I like to go riding early in the morning. A habit I picked up during my youth that I still enjoy today. I don't suppose you'd care to join me? I know you young men nowadays like to stay up all night gambling and whatnot and only return home as I'm heading out."

It was an obvious test of his character, and Kerrick smiled smoothly as he assumed the role of the perfect man for Rose Hardwick. "I'm not one for gambling," he said. "Not unless I know I can win. And I admit I haven't had as much opportunity to go riding as I'd like since I arrived in town."

"Splendid," Worthington said. If his wife hadn't been seated between them, Kerrick knew the man would have clapped him on the back. "Shall we say seven a.m. at Rotten Row? It should be quiet at that hour."

"I look forward to it," Kerrick said before rising and taking his leave.

When he returned to the Overlea box, Thornton was gone. The expression in Catherine's eyes when she met his was one of amusement, and in their depths he could all but see her assurance that he was the only one she saw as a romantic partner. He was glad she didn't view Thornton in that way, but that didn't make him dislike the man any less.

His mind more at ease now that he'd make plans to get closer to Worthington, Kerrick was able to enjoy the rest of the play. He'd read *The Taming of the Shrew* while at school but had never seen it performed. The thought had originally occurred to him that it would be nice to tame Catherine's impetuousness, but as he watched he found himself disturbed by the way Petruchio went about taming his shrewish wife. He couldn't help thinking that she hadn't been tamed— she'd been broken. Catherine might try his patience, but the very last thing he'd want was to see her spirit destroyed in the same way.

When the curtain lowered at the end of the fifth act, they remained in their box to avoid the crush of bodies moving to leave the theater at once. A few men came to their box to chat with Nicholas. Kerrick didn't miss the way his friend dragged his wife closer to his side as speculation entered the eyes of one man, well-known for his dalliances with married women of the *ton*, who was meeting the new Marchioness of Overlea for the first time.

Nicholas and Louisa's preoccupation gave him the opportunity to have a few moments alone with

Catherine as they moved to the other side of the box.

"Should I come by later tonight?" Her voice was pitched low so no one would overhear them.

Kerrick had to close his eyes for a moment as he struggled against the tide of lust that surged through him at the suggestion. When he opened them again, the eagerness in Catherine's eyes told him that she was in earnest. She'd actually risk her reputation and her safety to visit him again if he allowed it.

"Do that and I'll have to turn you over my knee," he said. That thought did nothing to help curb his desire as an image of Catherine, bared from the waist down and spread over his thighs, came to mind. The reproof, however, had Catherine pouting in disappointment.

"When?" she asked, clearly not content to let the matter drop.

"When this is all over."

Catherine's eyes moved to look over his shoulder, and he turned to find Nicholas had come up behind them. He had a moment of panic, afraid his friend had overhead the entire conversation, but his next words put that concern to rest.

"When what is all over?" he asked.

"The season," Kerrick said since he clearly couldn't have been talking about the play that had already ended. "Catherine was just asking me if I planned to visit Overlea Manor again. Of course, that would also depend on whether I'd still be welcome there."

Nicholas's gaze shifted to Catherine, then back to him.

"I suppose that would depend on how the rest of the spring goes. And on whether hearts are still intact."

Nicholas didn't have to say the words, but Kerrick heard the warning as clearly as if his friend had spoken. *Stop toying with Catherine's obvious affection for you.* He would like nothing better than to assure his friend that he wasn't toying with Catherine, and once again cursed the fact he wasn't in a position to do so.

CHAPTER NINE

KERRICK HAD HIGH hopes for his meeting with Worthington, but it wouldn't do to appear overeager, so he made sure to arrive exactly at the appointed hour the next morning. He noted with satisfaction that the other man was already waiting when he turned his mount on to the fashionable path in Hyde Park. At this early hour, though, the park was frequented mainly by grooms exercising the mounts of the aristocracy.

Worthington visibly puffed up when he caught sight of Kerrick. "It is an excellent morning to ride," he said by way of greeting when Kerrick's mount drew abreast.

And it was. The sun had chosen to make one of its rare appearances, setting the tone for what promised to be a pleasant day.

The horses trotted side by side for several minutes, the men saying very little, before Worthington turned the conversation to the subject that Kerrick knew was uppermost in his thoughts.

"I appreciate you doing me this courtesy." Worthington leaned toward him and lowered his voice before continuing. "Between the two of us, you must know that asking my permission to propose to Rose is only a formality. You will be so much better for her than those other boys who seek out her attention." The relief that accompanied those words was almost palpable.

Kerrick couldn't prevent the cynical thought that it was likely his own fortune that Worthington had his eye on. He inclined his head in acknowledgment of the compliment before going about his task of throwing the other man off guard. "I am not here to ask for permission to propose to your daughter."

Worthington tensed at his statement. He started to speak twice and had to stop before finally managing, "But you do intend to marry her? Everyone expects it, and to slight her would cause gossip. And we both know it is the dearest wish of your mother and Lady

Worthington."

Kerrick gritted his teeth against the rejoinder that everyone expected such a union only because Worthington was dropping hints in every ballroom and at every social event in London.

"I have no intention of causing your daughter any distress." His words were true because he was beginning to suspect that Rose Hardwick did not desire a union between them any more than he did. "You can rest assured that no negative gossip will arise from my actions toward Miss Hardwick. Watching her, however, it is very clear to me that she is enjoying her season very much. I wouldn't wish to take away from that enjoyment by declaring my intentions prematurely."

"A formal betrothal wouldn't end her enjoyment."

"Perhaps not, but I do have a confession to make."

The expression on the other man's face was a comical mixture of fear and hope, and Kerrick had to work to keep the corners of his mouth from lifting in amusement.

"I've never been fond of the social whirl."

He could hear the breath of relief that Worthington released at his statement.

"No man your age really is," Worthington rushed to say. "You're not yet thirty years of age, and I'm sure there are many more enjoyable ways you'd prefer to spend your evenings. I was a fan of gaming myself. But alas, once you have been married a few years…" He shrugged. "It's worse when you have a daughter. No way to stay away from all the events. But now and again you'll be able to drag yourself away and pursue your own interests. And fortunately no one expects a married man to dance attendance on his wife during all those balls."

Worthington must have realized he was babbling, for his mouth closed with an almost audible snap after his last pronouncement.

Kerrick couldn't help thinking about Nicholas and Clarington, who both seemed to enjoy staying at their wives' sides. Granted, they'd both been married less than a year, but Kerrick didn't see their behavior changing anytime soon. His thoughts went to Catherine and he knew he would never be content to sit in a card room while his wife danced with men whom he knew preyed upon the women who were feeling neglected by their spouses.

Ruthlessly he dragged his thoughts back to the present. He couldn't afford to allow himself to get distracted. If he didn't wind up this inquiry soon, he could end up finding himself a guest at Catherine's wedding to Viscount Thornton.

"I bow to your superior knowledge on the subject," Kerrick said, watching as Worthington preened visibly at the compliment. With a speed meant to throw the other man off balance, he changed the subject. "I didn't have the chance last night to ask who you were speaking to outside your box before the play began. You seemed overset by the meeting."

The color drained from Worthington's face and Kerrick felt a measure of satisfaction come to life within his chest. Brantford had been correct—Worthington was involved in something deep. But the question still remained as to whether it was also treasonous.

Worthington turned away and Kerrick could see he was struggling to regain his composure. His voice was tight when he replied.

"We always have so many visitors at these things when Rose is present... I can't recall one man in particular."

"Miss Hardwick wasn't yet upstairs at the time."

Worthington struggled for a few seconds before saying, "I do recall now what you mean. My wife had the headache. Before the play started I sought out a footman and asked him to bring a glass of water to the box."

Worthington was lying. The man he and Catherine had seen leaving the previous evening was no footman.

He longed to press the issue, but experience told him that nothing would be gained by pushing for information when a lighter hand would gain more results in the end. He had the confirmation he needed that Worthington was involved in something he didn't want anyone else discovering.

He wondered if the man's wife knew about it and his mind started churning with how he could pursue that line of inquiry. At the back of his mind, the thought surfaced that Catherine's new friendship with Rose placed her in the perfect position to make discreet inquiries of Rose's mother, but he refused to give that possibility any serious consideration. The very last thing he wanted was Catherine involved further in this mess. She'd placed herself there, but he would do whatever he could to make sure she didn't take any risks. Lord and Lady Worthington were not the dangerous sort, but he knew from other missions that desperate people would often act out of character to protect themselves. And if the safety of their family was involved... No, he definitely wouldn't ask Catherine to involve herself in this.

"I hope that Lady Worthington was feeling better this morning."

Worthington's whole demeanor relaxed at the change in subject. "She was still abed when I left.

Unfortunately, her headaches are a more common occurrence than she would like, but normally they pass after a night of rest. I thank you for your concern."

Kerrick gave the other man a smile aimed at putting him at ease. "I am very glad to hear that. Will she be well enough to attend the Hastings' rout this evening?"

Worthington shook his head. "She normally likes a quiet evening at home after one of her episodes, especially if they occur during an evening out." His relief that the subject had returned to safer ground was almost palpable.

"I can't say that I blame her," Kerrick said. "Since most of these evenings are interminable in the best of circumstances, I can't imagine having to endure one while feeling unwell."

Worthington laughed, his normally effusive nature once more at the forefront. "That is where we men are very different from women. I fear very little keeps them from spending every evening out during the season. If she didn't think tonight's event would turn into a way to showcase the musical talents of Lady Hastings' daughters, she would force herself to go no matter how badly she felt."

Kerrick didn't have to feign his look of horror. He'd already had the misfortune of hearing the eldest daughter mangle her way through Bach. "They wouldn't."

"Consider yourself warned. Of course, Lady Hastings already knows your attention lies elsewhere, so I'm sure you'll be safe."

THE CARRIAGE STOPPED before the milliner's shop on Bond Street at precisely ten in the morning, and Catherine stepped down, her maid following behind her. When she didn't see Rose, Catherine wondered if the other woman had changed her mind about meeting her. The note she'd received a short time ago had said Rose was already on her way out of the house, so she should have been there.

Catherine was torn about whether to send the carriage away and wait on the street or climb back inside and return home. Rose's note had seemed important, however, so she told the driver to return in half an hour. As the carriage started to move away, she was relieved to see Rose emerge from a nearby dress shop, her own maid in tow. That relief changed to worry when she took in the tightness of her friend's features.

"I'm so glad you were able to meet me on such short notice," Rose said, grasping her hands quickly and giving them a slight squeeze before dropping them again. "I wasn't sure you'd be able to come."

"My mornings are normally free," Catherine said, thinking about how her sister was even now lying in bed, suffering from the unsettled stomach so often seen in newly pregnant women. "Your note seemed urgent. Is something the matter?"

"Walk with me a bit," Rose said, taking Catherine's arm in hers and starting to stroll down the street at a leisurely pace.

Their maids fell into step behind them. Rose must have already told hers that she wanted privacy because the two women stayed several steps back from them. Catherine wondered what could possibly have happened to warrant the concern on her friend's face. After all, she'd seen her just the evening before and all had seemed well.

"You are beginning to worry me," Catherine said.

Rose gave a humorless laugh. "I apologize. I can see how dramatic I'm being, but I was truly concerned and needed to speak with you right away."

"Has something happened?"

Rose shook her head. "Not yet, but I fear it is about to." She ignored those who looked their way and would have no doubt stopped to chat if Rose had shown the slightest inclination that she would welcome the intrusion. When she continued, her voice was barely audible. "When my maid woke me this morning, she told me that Father had gone riding with Lord Kerrick."

Catherine didn't have to feign her surprise. Kerrick hadn't mentioned anything to her about going riding with Lord Worthington, but they hadn't had much time to converse in private. She also suspected he hadn't mentioned the meeting to her because he was still quite adamant about not involving her in his investigations. She would just have to show him how much help she could be to him.

"I am sure Lord Kerrick regularly goes riding." As the words escaped her lips, her thoughts went back to the night they had spent together, and she had to turn away to hide the heat she could feel creeping into her cheeks. Fortunately, Rose was too preoccupied to notice.

"Perhaps, but Father likes to ride alone in the morning. He enjoys the solitude and the exercise. If he planned to meet with Lord Kerrick, I know it is because Father hopes he will ask for permission to propose marriage."

Catherine knew that was unlikely to happen—or at least she hoped that was the case—but she couldn't tell Rose that her worries were unfounded.

"What will you do if Lord Kerrick proposes?"

Rose gave her a look of disbelief. "I'll reject him, of

course. He seems very nice and he is very attractive…"

"But you have feelings for your mysterious man."

A whisper of a smile touched Rose's lips. "It is hopeless, I know. And I have mostly come to terms with that reality. But if I were to accept Lord Kerrick, I would make the lives of three people miserable. Aside from myself, I couldn't do that to you or to him because it is obvious to me that he returns your affection."

There was nothing Catherine could say in reply. She only hoped it wasn't as obvious to others, because Kerrick needed to remain on good terms with Lord Worthington.

Rose's thoughts must have gone back to the other man, because while she tried to hide it, Catherine could see her despair. Her heart went out to the other woman. If something happened to keep her and Kerrick apart, she didn't know if she'd be able to bear it.

"How would your father react if you turned down a marriage proposal from Lord Kerrick?"

Rose waited to reply until they passed a young woman and what must have been her mother coming out of a dressmaker's shop. When no one was near, she said, "He wouldn't be happy, and I fear he would do what he could to change my mind."

The stark tone in her voice had Catherine frowning. "He would force you to accept?"

"Until recently I never would have thought him the type of father to force me into a marriage I do not desire, but now…" She sighed. "Yes, I believe he would."

A shiver of unease went down Catherine's spine at the thought. Her sister had been in a similar position the previous year—agreeing to marry the Marquess of Overlea to secure all their futures—but from the beginning it was clear she was attracted to Nicholas. Their marriage had been shaky at the start because of Nicholas's illness, but in the end everything had worked out, and now they were the happiest married couple Catherine knew. She couldn't imagine what it would be like to marry one man while in love with a different one. And if she were being completely truthful, she did not want to even contemplate a future where Rose and Kerrick were married.

"Why does he desire this match so much? It would not be exaggerating to say that you could have any man you want." When Rose frowned, Catherine continued, "I don't know who your mysterious man is, but I'm sure he wouldn't be immune to your charms if you decided to set your cap for him."

Rose looked away. "Lord Kerrick is immune."

Catherine sincerely hoped that was true. "Fine, then. Almost any man. Is not one of the men in your group of admirers the heir to the Marquess of Cranley?"

"Yes, but his family is not as wealthy as Lord Kerrick."

Given her own family's recent poverty, Catherine could well understand the motives behind Lord Worthington's desire to secure his daughter's future.

"I'm sorry. I didn't realize wealth was a consideration."

Rose pulled her into the small space between two shops and indicated to their maids that they should wait on the other side of the street before she turned to face Catherine again.

"That is what I least understand. A few years ago we were in a bad way. Two years ago, Mama talked to me about how I probably would not receive a season. But then things changed. Mama said something about certain improvements Father had made and that our income had increased as a result."

The hair at the back of Catherine's neck rose. The Worthingtons had undergone a sudden increase in fortune. Until that moment, she'd been hoping to learn that Kerrick was wrong and that Lord Worthington was innocent of whatever he suspected he'd done. But if there was one thing Catherine had learned, it was to trust her instincts. And right now her instincts were telling her that there was more to this change in the Worthingtons' fortunes than improvements being made to their estate.

"That is most interesting," she said, her voice carefully neutral. "Did you ever learn what was done?"

The look Rose aimed at her told her that her friend thought she had lost her mind.

"Father doesn't discuss the running of the estate with me. In any case, that is beside the point. Two years ago I would have understood his desire to see me marry a man with a title and a wealthy estate behind him. But now?" She shook her head. "It makes no sense to me. We haven't been lacking for anything, and while I know he wants to see me marry well, there are many other men who could provide for me in a more-than-adequate fashion. I don't understand why he's so insistent that I concentrate all my attention on securing Lord Kerrick's interest."

"Was there not an understanding between your mother and Lord Kerrick's? I overheard him say something about the two being very good friends."

Rose shrugged. "Yes, they imagined a future where the families would one day be united, but there was never a formal betrothal between us... Thank heavens!"

That would explain why Kerrick was so willing to pursue a future with her instead of Rose. But that still didn't solve their current predicament. Catherine was at a complete loss as to how she could help turn the current situation to the advantage of all of them.

"This man who has captured your interest… does he have no money?"

Rose laughed, the sound filled with genuine amusement, but there was a hollowness behind it. "He puts even Lord Kerrick's wealth to shame. But since he rarely so much as glances in my direction, I can hardly count on his interest putting my father off from trying to make sure Lord Kerrick and I are wed before the year is over."

That news startled Catherine. "This is your first season, surely there is no hurry."

Rose shook her head. "I don't understand his urgency, but I fear he is quite determined to see us wed very soon."

Catherine wanted to assure her that would never happen, but she couldn't stop a hint of doubt from creeping into her own mind. What if Kerrick tired of her as he had the many other women he'd been with? They'd made love, but that was no guarantee that he would stay with her. Especially since no one knew about their liaison. Of course, if she let it slip to Louisa, she had no doubt that Nicholas would make sure that his friend offered for her. But was that what she wanted? To force Kerrick's hand? And would he come to hate her if she did? The thought sat heavy in her belly, creating an almost fathomless pit of despair at the possibility.

"Catherine, did you hear what I said?"

Rose's hand on her arm, shaking her gently, roused her from her thoughts.

"I'm sorry," she said, hoping her apologetic smile didn't appear as empty as it felt.

"I understand," Rose said, squeezing her hand before releasing it. "I imagine the thought of Lord Kerrick and me marrying is quite as unpleasant to you as it is to me. That is why we must make sure it will never come to pass."

The look of determination on Rose's face had Catherine afraid to ask what she meant. "And how will we do that?"

"We must make sure that everyone realizes it is you Lord Kerrick cares for and not me. And if we're lucky, perhaps we can get him to compromise you."

Her words, so close to the thoughts that had just been going through her own mind, had Catherine almost reeling in shock.

"No, we can't…"

"Of course we can. In fact, we must. I'm sure that between the two of us we can manage it."

Now that she had decided on a plan of action, Rose was back to being her lighter, carefree self. It was a facade, of course, but it was clear that Rose's resolution to see her and Kerrick together had filled her with new life. Catherine, on the other hand, was filled with dread at this new turn of events. Kerrick was not going to be happy when he learned of Rose's plan.

CHAPTER TEN

WHEN BRANTFORD WAS in town, he made it a point to visit White's daily to cement his reputation as an idle member of the aristocracy. It also allowed him the opportunity to meet with many of his connections without calling undue attention to himself. Many sought out his company just for the prestige of being seen with him, which meant no one thought it unusual for Kerrick to approach him there.

Kerrick crossed the sumptuously decorated front room and stopped at the entrance to the salon where Brantford was sprawled in a winged armchair. The other man noticed him right away—there wasn't much that escaped his attention. With only a casual glance from Brantford, the two men he'd been speaking to rose from their chairs and moved away, allowing Kerrick the privacy he needed for this meeting. He had no idea how Brantford did it, but he'd long since given up trying to guess who was on the payroll of the Home Office and who was merely trying to curry favor with the holder of one of the oldest and wealthiest titles in all of England.

"Worthington is definitely hiding something," Kerrick said after taking one of the vacated seats.

"And good afternoon to you."

There was a sharpness to his tone that had Kerrick pausing to examine the other man. Brantford had assumed his usual pose, leaning back in his chair, a half-empty snifter of brandy dangling from his fingers—one that Kerrick knew wouldn't be refilled—but something was wrong. He couldn't say how he knew since the other man had always been impossible to read. Today was no different, but somehow he knew that Brantford was not happy to see him.

"Did I interrupt something important?"

Brantford raised a brow. "With Bryers and Carlson? Definitely not."

Well, this was an interesting occurrence. It wasn't often that Kerrick was witness to Brantford's feathers being ruffled. He leaned forward, bracing his elbows on his knees as he made no effort to hide his examination of the other man.

"Is there something you'd like to share with me?"

Brantford's eyes narrowed. It was almost imperceptible, and Kerrick would have missed it if he hadn't been watching him closely.

"And here I thought you had information to share with me."

The corner of Kerrick's mouth lifted. "Anything I could possibly have to share with you can wait. What I want to know is why the Unaffected Earl is showing himself to be less than aloof."

A hint of something that might have been amusement lit Brantford's eyes. "Much as I am enjoying this conversation, I fear I have another appointment and must be leaving soon."

Kerrick released an exaggerated sigh. "And we were having so much fun bantering."

"You were bantering," Brantford said, his neutral mask once again firmly in place. "I was enduring."

"You are, of course, completely correct. I fear I must be losing my touch. It might be best if you found someone else to replace me."

"Soon, Kerrick. After you complete this last mission."

He sobered at the reminder. That time could not come soon enough for him.

"At the theater last night I happened to see Worthington returning to his theater box, but he wasn't himself. He never loses an opportunity to stop and speak to me, but yesterday he brushed by me and was visibly shaken. I think he was returning from a meeting, but I couldn't identify the person he was speaking to. He was too far away and headed in the opposite direction before melding into the crowd. There were too many people around to attempt to give chase."

"Pity," Brantford said.

"Yes. I arranged to go riding with Worthington this morning, and when I mentioned it, he was visibly shaken. Tried to say he was speaking to a footman."

"So our suspicions about him appear to be correct."

"Yes." He barely refrained from swearing.

Brantford's eyes narrowed. "You appear to be upset."

Kerrick shrugged. "This won't end well. If we uncover that Worthington is involved with passing on secrets, his entire family will be ruined. His wife and daughter don't deserve that."

Brantford was silent for an unusually long time. When he spoke, he said simply, "No, I don't suppose that they do."

Kerrick straightened and rested his head against the back of the chair. "I can't wait to be finished with this whole line of work. I can't imagine why I ever enjoyed it."

"If memory serves, you were quite eager to help your country when I approached you."

"I was also young and stupid."

"You've been a great asset and will be missed."

The compliment took him aback. For Brantford, it was almost effusive. Kerrick inclined his head and waited, sensing that something of great importance was coming. His instincts were rarely wrong, and they did not fail him now.

"How is your courtship of Miss Hardwick progressing?"

Brantford had been occupied with casting his eye over the room when he asked the casual question, but Kerrick zeroed in on the action for what it was. The question was of great importance to the man sitting opposite him, affecting the appearance of one who held only the slightest interest in the subject at hand. It was a tactic Brantford often used to draw attention away from just how interested he was in the answer.

Kerrick's eyes never left the other man's face as he replied, his tone equally casual. "I believe Miss

Hardwick possesses depths that she tries very hard to keep hidden from others. And I've discovered that I like her."

Brantford's hand paused for only the briefest of seconds as he drew his watch from a pocket to glance at the time.

Kerrick waited until he'd returned the watch before continuing. "The whole world believes we will be announcing our betrothal at any moment. Given the expectations of society and my own family, I've been considering whether I should continue to court her in earnest."

Kerrick wanted to crow with triumph when Brantford's jaw tightened. "I take it that wouldn't meet with your approval?"

Brantford's gaze settled squarely on him. "I fail to see what your personal relationships have to do with me. But won't Miss Evans be disappointed?"

Kerrick refused to be baited into changing the subject. "I know, Brantford." He was bluffing, but every one of his instincts was telling him that the Unaffected Earl had feelings for Rose Hardwick.

"If I find any information that would be of use to you in your investigation, I'll make sure to pass it along. Until then, I have an appointment I can't miss."

Brantford placed his drink on a side table, stood,

and without another word strode from the room. His lack of response told Kerrick everything he needed to know.

SHE'D ONLY BEEN to one rout before that evening, but Catherine found she far preferred them to the formal balls and musical evenings. The smaller house parties were more intimate and, to her, far more enjoyable. She'd been relieved after learning from Rose that her family wouldn't be in attendance. She didn't know if Kerrick would be there, but if he was she wouldn't have to watch him pay court to someone else. Even though she knew the truth of the situation, it was difficult watching her every step and taking care not to spend too much time in his company. But surely with the Worthingtons not in attendance, and with everyone aware of the great friendship between Kerrick and Nicholas, no one would look twice if she allowed herself to enjoy his company.

She did feel a little twinge of guilt about Louisa. Normally the sickness that held her sister in its grips during the morning hours would have disappeared by the evening. And Louisa took a nap most afternoons so that she would be refreshed for their evening entertainments. Catherine couldn't help but notice, however, that her sister wasn't her usual self that evening. But since Louisa hadn't said anything about not attending the rout, and because she had so been looking forward to going, she hadn't asked Louisa if she wanted to stay home. A good sister, one who wasn't acting selfishly, would have asked if her somewhat haggard-looking sibling was feeling up to going out. Louisa had always tended to sacrifice far too much for her family, and Catherine couldn't ignore her suspicion that she was doing the same right now. The fact that Nicholas was being more attentive than normal supported that belief.

She told herself that if Kerrick didn't show soon, she'd insist they go home.

When Kerrick walked into the Hastings' drawing room shortly after their own arrival, looking particularly handsome in black and a waistcoat of royal blue that mirrored the color of his eyes, her guilt only increased because she knew they wouldn't be leaving early. She tried to squelch the feeling by reasoning that her sister would never put her pregnancy at risk and could decide for herself if she needed to leave.

His gaze swept across the room and halted when he saw her. He didn't smile, but she could see the satisfaction in his eyes. Aware that Louisa was looking at her and that her sister knew her almost better than she knew herself, she looked away from him.

"Lord Kerrick is here," Louisa said.

Her sister saw far too much. Out of everyone she knew, Catherine found it most difficult to know how to behave around her when Kerrick's name came up in conversation. Louisa already knew her feelings for him went beyond friendship—Catherine had hardly been subtle about it in the past—so she couldn't pretend disinterest now. But how could she be her normal self around the man and not betray that their relationship had gone a step further? Louisa and Nicholas must never suspect.

As she struggled to think of what to say to her sister, she was glad that Nicholas had gone to fetch them drinks. For whatever reason, he was very protective of her.

In the end, she opted for brevity. "Yes," she said simply, allowing her smile of happiness to show. To do less would be to arouse her sister's suspicions.

They stood off to the side of the room, and when she glanced up, she saw him approaching. Awareness, sharp and swift, went through her and she found it impossible to look away again. To his credit, he did stop and speak to a group of men first so he wouldn't appear too anxious to see her. But she knew otherwise.

Louisa grasped her hand and Catherine turned her attention back to her sister.

"Please remember that his interest lies elsewhere," Louisa said.

Relief went through her at the confirmation that her sister didn't suspect there was already more between her and Kerrick.

She couldn't promise her sister that she would relinquish all interest in Kerrick, so instead she said, "I don't recall a betrothal announcement going out? Was it in this morning's paper and no one told me?"

Louisa sighed in exasperation and Catherine laughed.

"You are truly incorrigible," her sister said.

"We already knew that."

Catherine looked up to see Kerrick had disentangled himself from his friends and now stood before them. Amusement lit his eyes and she knew he was remembering a certain brazen encounter that she had initiated not two days before. She didn't know what to say but was saved when Nicholas returned with their drinks. She thanked him and took a sip of the ratafia.

Kerrick turned his attention to Louisa. "You look beautiful as ever, Lady Overlea."

Louisa's smile was quick, but behind it Catherine could detect signs of strain. Another wave of guilt swept through her when Nicholas took Louisa's arm and she smiled up at him in relief.

"Perhaps we should sit down. My wife is feeling a little under the weather tonight. On my way back I saw one of the card tables was free. We could venture to see if that's still the case."

Nicholas didn't wait for their response but turned and started for the morning room where tables had been set out for those guests who wanted to play.

Kerrick offered Catherine his arm, and when she took it, warmth flooded through her. It took every ounce of her will not to sink against him and bask in his closeness. The way the fingers of his other hand tightened briefly over hers where it lay on his arm told her that he would enjoy nothing more. But instead they kept a circumspect distance apart while they followed Louisa and Nicholas into the morning room.

As they passed through the hallway, Catherine was happy to see that the Duke and Duchess of Clarington had just arrived. The way Lord and Lady Hastings greeted the pair, however, told her that it would likely be some time before they would be able to extricate themselves from the host and hostess.

Since everyone's attention was on the newly arrived pair, Catherine paused and looked up at Kerrick. "I need to speak to you," she said under her breath, the words barely audible.

"I don't think—"

"I was with Rose this morning. She told me something you should know."

He nodded but said nothing as a group passed them. They moved forward again, and when they entered the morning room she saw that her brother-in-law had managed to secure the open card table. Nicholas was sitting across from Louisa, holding her hands in his, and as she and Kerrick approached she overheard him urging her sister to go home.

She could no longer ignore her guilt. Taking a seat between them, she turned to Louisa. "If you're not feeling well, we can leave."

Her sister shook her head. "Nonsense. Nicholas is just being overly protective."

"I'm being the right amount of protective," Nicholas said with a frown. "You push yourself too much."

Louisa gave him a fond smile and turned to Catherine. "I will be fine. If I become overtired, I will let everyone know. Until that point, shall we play?"

Kerrick took that moment to interject. "Is there something I should know?"

Catherine made sure not to meet his eyes as he asked the question. He was aware of Louisa's pregnancy because she had let the information slip, but a formal announcement had yet to be made. He kept a straight face though when Nicholas relayed the news that they were expecting a happy event in the fall.

"Is the father someone I know?" Kerrick asked, raising a brow.

Catherine couldn't hold back her surprised gasp at the suggestion her sister would betray her husband. She was even more shocked, however, when Louisa laughed outright.

"You're terrible."

Nicholas scowled. "It's far too soon for such jokes," he said. His annoyance was clear, but he wasn't as angry as such a suggestion should have made him.

The glance her brother-in-law cast in her direction, however, made her aware, once again, that something existed between the other three. Something they'd taken great pains to keep hidden from her. Louisa's amusement at what anyone else would consider an insult was clear proof that Kerrick and her sister were on much friendlier terms than they should be. But it was Nicholas's lack of reaction that puzzled her the most. Any other man would have been demanding that Kerrick meet him at dawn for delivering such an insult to his wife.

They settled on a game of whist. Despite Louisa's assurances that she felt well, it was clear that her mind wasn't completely on their game when she missed several opportunities to win a trick. Nicholas was scarcely better. He was so concerned about his wife that he barely looked at his own cards. It was no wonder then that Catherine and Kerrick won the first hand with scarcely any effort.

Louisa tried but couldn't hold back her yawn and Nicholas threw down the cards he still held. The look on his face told her that the evening was at an end and that he would brook no denial. Louisa didn't even try.

"I'm sorry. I don't know why I'm such poor company tonight. I didn't rise until almost noon."

Catherine had hoped to find an opportunity during the evening to speak to Kerrick alone—or as alone as one could be in a room filled with other people—but she couldn't force her sister to stay when it appeared as though she might fall asleep at any moment. She would just have to leave it to him to find a way to speak to her soon.

"I should have insisted we stay home tonight," she said. "It was very selfish of me to make you come out tonight when I could see that you were tired."

"Perhaps I can suggest an alternative."

They all turned to look at Kerrick, who was leaning back in his seat, his arms folded across his chest.

"The Claringtons arrived just as we were leaving the drawing room. I'm sure the duchess wouldn't mind acting as Miss Evans's chaperone for the remainder of the evening."

Catherine turned to her sister, unable to hide her eagerness at the proposition. "Do you think that would be fine? We had fun when we went to Kew Gardens. She might not think it too much of an imposition."

"I don't see why not," Louisa said. "If she doesn't mind, I could then go home without feeling as though I had spoiled all your fun."

Nicholas nodded briskly. "I'll go speak to Clarington now. I don't want to place the duchess in an awkward position by asking her directly if they have plans to go elsewhere tonight."

He was gone only a few minutes, but when he returned he wasn't alone. The Duke and Duchess of Clarington were with him. Charlotte went straight for Louisa and gave her a quick hug.

"Overlea told us the good news. I would be very happy to stay with Catherine tonight."

"If you are certain. I do not wish to impose—" Louisa started.

"It is no imposition at all. In fact, Catherine and I have some catching up to do since we last spoke, and I want to hear all about how she is enjoying London."

The gleam in the duchess's eyes left Catherine in no doubt what she wished to speak to her about. Charlotte wanted to know if she'd managed to ensnare Kerrick's interest. Catherine didn't want to lie to her, but she couldn't tell her the truth.

Her mind at ease that a suitable chaperone had been found, Louisa allowed Nicholas to take her home. The rest of the evening passed in a blur of music and dancing, followed by a late supper. When the duchess told her that she and her husband would be leaving soon, Catherine still hadn't found a moment to tell Kerrick about Rose's plans to throw the two of them together at every opportunity.

She looked around to see if she could catch one final glimpse of him, but he seemed to have vanished. She tried to quell her disappointment. Kerrick knew she needed to speak with him privately, and she had to believe that he'd find a way to make that happen soon. If not that night, then perhaps he'd visit their town house on the morrow.

As she left the Hastings' home with the Duke and Duchess of Clarington, she noticed absently that the carriage awaiting them was not the same one they'd taken on their last outing together. That one had been larger and had born Clarington's ducal crest, but this one was bare of all markings. She reasoned that the Claringtons no doubt had several carriages and perhaps they used this one when they didn't wish to attract too much attention.

Charlotte settled beside her in the carriage while Clarington took the seat opposite her. She had only a moment to wonder at the curious expression on his face when the duchess spoke. "What exactly is between you and Lord Kerrick?"

Not expecting the question, especially not in front of the duke, Catherine floundered for a response. She didn't wish to lie, but she couldn't compromise the trust Kerrick had placed in her.

"He is a very good friend."

Charlotte was not about to let her evade the question. "You're fond of him and wish to become closer. Despite the fact that he is openly courting another woman."

Clarington had remained silent, but the weight of his gaze seemed to settle heavily over her. Embarrassed, Catherine closed her eyes and wished fervently for a hole to open up on the carriage floor so she could escape. The duchess meant well, but she and her husband must truly think her pathetic. She half expected to receive a lecture about how she should let go of her foolish fantasies. She'd originally thought that Kerrick being a spy was exciting and romantic, but in that moment she hated what he was. Hated that she was forced to lie to everyone and that they no doubt saw her as a delusional, silly girl.

"I don't wish to discuss this—"

The duke cut her off. "Given what is about to happen, not answering Charlotte's question isn't an option."

The undercurrent of anger in his words surprised her. She watched, dumbfounded, as Charlotte reached over and laid a hand on her husband's knee, an action that was clearly meant to signal that he should leave the questions to her. Clarington gave her a dark look but said nothing more.

"Do you care for Lord Kerrick?" Charlotte asked.

Since it was clear they weren't about to let her evade the question, she had no choice but to answer.

"Yes," Catherine said simply. They could think what they would, but she wouldn't deny her feelings.

Her answer seemed to satisfy Charlotte, though, and she shot a triumphant look toward her husband.

"Alex isn't happy about this, but I, for one, have always believed in love. If I hadn't… well, we wouldn't be married now."

"This is not at all the same situation," Clarington said.

"Perhaps not, but I've learned that sometimes you need to take a risk if you love someone."

Clarington's face softened as he looked at his wife,

and it was clear to Catherine that he loved her very much.

The carriage stopped at that moment and she was surprised when a footman opened the door. They couldn't be home already, a suspicion that was confirmed when she looked out the door. They appeared to be in a darkened street, one which Catherine did not recognize.

"Why are we stopping?"

Charlotte smiled and, to Catherine's shock, allowed the footman to help her down from the carriage. Clarington aimed a serious look her way.

"Nicholas trusts me, and I sincerely hope I am not making a gross error in judgment." He gave his head a sharp shake, his expression one of fond bemusement. "Charlotte is having a terrible effect on me."

With that cryptic statement, he, too, descended from the carriage. Catherine sat there in shock, unsure what to do. Did they expect her to follow them? But in the next moment everything became clear when Kerrick swung into the carriage, closed the door behind him, and settled into the seat Clarington had just vacated.

Pure joy swept through her as she realized he must have made arrangements with the duke and duchess for them to have this moment of privacy. Anticipation was a steady thrum in her veins as the carriage started forward again. Here, where no one could see them, she allowed her feelings free rein as she drank in the sight of him.

CHAPTER ELEVEN

HE WAS GOING to burn in hell for this—right after Nicholas called him out. It had only been two days since Catherine had come to his house. Two days since he had vowed to keep his distance from her. And yet here he was, already making excuses to see her again in private. He could have taken a moment to pull her aside during the evening. There would have been nothing improper in having a private conversation a few feet away from others but within their sight. Everyone knew of his friendship with Catherine's brother-in-law. As long as he kept a respectable distance between them, no one would have raised a brow. But he hadn't been able to resist the temptation of arranging for this private rendezvous. He hadn't had so little self-control since he was a youth.

Seeing her now, happiness shining on her face, he knew it would be next to impossible to keep his desire for her in check. In the enclosed space of the dark carriage, the exotic scent of her perfume curled around him. He wanted nothing more than to pull her onto his lap and continue from where they'd left off the last time they'd been alone together.

Catherine had said she needed to speak to him about something Rose Hardwick had told her. He needed to keep his mind on the task at hand if he was to conclude his mission and extricate himself from his current romantic entanglement with Rose.

Catherine leaned forward. "How did you …?" She stopped abruptly and heat crept up her face. "Does Clarington know about us? About what happened?"

Reaching out, he captured one of her hands and shook his head. "I have told no one—you know I wouldn't speak of what happened between us. Not when everyone must believe I am pursuing Rose Hardwick."

"The duchess knows about my feelings for you. She might have told him."

For a moment he expected the worst, but he had to

find out just how much Catherine had revealed. "You didn't tell her—"

"No," Catherine said with a firm shake of her head. "I promised you I wouldn't tell anyone about what you are doing. And if anyone knew about that night…" She stopped, pulled her hand from his, and straightened in her seat. "It wouldn't be prudent for me to expose what happened. I know many would think nothing of trapping a man into offering for them, but I am not one of those women. In any case, we both know you are not free even if I were the type to scheme in such a way."

Annoyance flared to life within him. Did she really believe he was the type of man to just leave her to suffer from a ruined reputation? His current line of inquiry could go to the devil if anyone learned that he had taken her innocence. Even if she weren't Louisa's sister, his sense of honor would never allow him to behave in such a cavalier manner.

Another, more unsettling thought occurred to him. Did Catherine believe he was just trifling with her? He'd had his share of amorous liaisons over the years, but only with experienced women who knew their trysts would go no further. He'd never debauched an innocent, and it bothered him more than he could say that she'd believe him capable of such a thing.

Two lines formed between her brows. "Is something the matter?"

He realized that he was frowning and drew upon his years of practice at concealing his thoughts to smooth out his expression. He refused to consider his suspicion that he was acting more on emotion than intellect, something he could not afford to do until this whole mess was over. Only then could he turn his attention fully to the beguiling creature before him.

"You said you had something important to tell me about your meeting with Miss Hardwick this morning."

For a moment he thought she wasn't going to allow him to evade her question, but in the end she didn't pursue it.

"You won't be pleased to hear this… it places your investigation at risk."

"What happened?" he asked, his mind jumping to the worst possible scenario, that he'd tipped his hand that morning when he'd questioned Worthington about his upset the previous night at the theater.

"I didn't say anything to Rose, but she's very observant. She's guessed that I have feelings for you."

He began to breathe a little easier with her admission. "You haven't hidden the fact that you have a *tendre* for me."

Her shoulders stiffened, telling him that he'd annoyed her, but he couldn't understand why. From the way everyone acted, her affection for him was widely known. He only hoped that affection wouldn't turn to someone else before this whole business was behind them.

"That may well be, my lord spymaster extraordinaire, but it will surprise you to know that you haven't been any more successful in keeping you own feelings hidden."

That wiped the smile from his face. "What, exactly, are you saying?"

"Rose has guessed that you return my affections."

His thoughts immediately went back to the previous evening and the way Rose had seemed at ease with him at the theater—more at ease than she'd ever been in his presence—and he realized Catherine was speaking the truth. Not that she'd have any reason to lie to him about such a thing.

He swore and leaned back against the carriage seat as he contemplated the repercussions of Catherine's revelation.

She rose from her seat and crossed the small space that separated them to sit beside him. He turned his head to look at her and was surprised at the concern in her eyes.

"I promise that I didn't betray your confidence. She guessed."

He straightened and reached to take the hand that hovered over his arm. Her hesitation to touch him bothered him more than he wanted to admit.

"I know, Catherine. If you had slipped, you would tell me."

Her head tilted and even in the darkness he could see that her eyes had brightened.

"You trust me."

He squeezed her hand in answer. "I'm not happy you've embroiled yourself in this, and I still hope to convince you to distance yourself from the Worthingtons, but only because I worry for your safety. I trust you not to reveal anything I've told you."

She shook her head as though unable to believe his words. "Louisa still thinks of me as her baby sister and acts as though she needs to shelter me from the world."

"Your sister is almost eight years older than you and has looked after you since your mother died in your infancy. She will always see you as her younger sister and will want to protect you. But in case you haven't noticed, I see you as the beautiful, intelligent young woman you are."

Their eyes met and held. Kerrick was a hairsbreadth away from pouncing on her when she looked away and said, her voice faint, "There's more. Rose has decided to play the matchmaker between us."

"Of course she has." The entire situation was so ridiculous that he couldn't hold back a quick bark of laughter. "God save me from romantic females. How am I supposed to continue to pay court to her when she will be trying to throw the two of us together?"

Catherine's mouth turned up. "It is most decidedly a complication."

"That, my dear, is a vast understatement." His amusement died as he realized that he needed to stop allowing himself to be distracted by his affection for Catherine. He had to start paying more attention to his latest—and hopefully his last—mission. "We cannot risk being caught together."

She released a soft sigh. "I know. And when we attend the same functions, we must be careful to keep our distance. Rose is quite taken with her new plan to see if she can make us a couple."

Their hands were still joined and he raised them to place a kiss on her palm. Her breath quickened at the intimate caress.

"This might be the last time we'll be alone together for some time. I will do everything in my power to end this investigation quickly, but these things do not always go according to plan."

Her tongue darted across her lips and his entire body tightened in response.

"We shouldn't waste this opportunity," she said, tracing the line of his jaw with her other hand.

He could no sooner deny the desire to have her in his arms than he could resist the need to draw his next breath. When he grasped her waist to haul her onto his lap, he'd intended to have her sit her sideways, a halfhearted attempt to fool himself into thinking that he was still in control of this encounter. But she would have none of it and surprised him by lifting her dress and moving so that she straddled him.

Their lips were almost touching, and despite the fact that nothing had yet happened between them, they were already breathing heavily.

"You, Miss Evans, are a delightful surprise," he managed before taking her mouth with his own.

He wanted to take his time to enjoy this moment with her, but at the back of his mind was the ever-present knowledge that this encounter would soon draw to a close. When he'd made arrangements with the Claringtons to have Catherine brought to his carriage, he'd instructed the driver to take a roundabout way to Overlea's town house. But he hadn't wanted to risk Catherine's reputation by prolonging the trip by more than ten minutes, fifteen at most. That didn't leave much time before this brief interlude would be over.

Catherine must have sensed his urgency, for the desperation of her kiss seemed to match his own. He kept his hands planted on her hips, telling himself he'd have to be content with the feel of her slight weight leaning against him as the mouths and tongues moved together.

The heat that rose in the confined space of the carriage threatened to engulf him. He honestly couldn't say who moved first, but within moments her body was pressed against the length of his, her legs squeezing against his hips while she pressed intimately against his erection. The soft mewling sounds she made as she rocked against him threatened to drive him to madness.

He couldn't take her again—they'd already risked too much when she'd spent the night with him—but that didn't mean he couldn't give her pleasure.

Gritting his teeth to keep his need to thrust into her in check, he lowered her bodice as she continued to rock against him. Because her décolletage was low, she wore a half-corset below the sky-blue gown. Within moments he'd freed her breasts and drew one tight nipple into his mouth. One hand caressed her breast while the other tightened against her hip. The catch in her voice as she approached her peak had him struggling against the almost overwhelming need to throw her onto her back and bury himself within her.

"Kerrick... oh..."

She froze and he watched her, enthralled, as her orgasm swept over her. On the verge of spilling himself in his trousers like a youth, he planted his hands against her hips and pushed her lower body away from his. She murmured in protest and tried to sink back against him, but he held her lower body firmly at a distance.

She reached down to touch him. He closed his eyes for several seconds while her fingers cradled his shaft, squeezing lightly. A war raged within him. He was on the verge of giving in to his need for her when two loud knocks shattered the moment—his coachman's signal that they were only two minutes from Overlea's town house.

Kerrick cursed and shifted Catherine off his lap. When he moved to take the seat opposite her, she gazed at him with dazed befuddlement. Her breasts were still spilling over the top of her dress and her hair had come half down. He groaned and tore his eyes away lest he throw her onto her back and finish what they had started.

"We'll be at your door soon, and unless you mean to enter the house in that manner, you'd better..." He waved a hand in the direction of her bodice and couldn't avoid looking at her again.

The warning served to snap Catherine out of her confusion, and in quick order she drew her dress back into place and smoothed down her skirts. She was working on pinning her hair up when he spoke.

"I'm going to call on Miss Hardwick tomorrow afternoon. I'm sure her parents will encourage her to accept a drive with me to Hyde Park."

Catherine's hands stilled, but only for a moment. "I think that's wise. We can only hope her parents are not nearly as observant as Rose, but in case they suspect there is something between us, it will go a long way to cementing your relationship with them if you make a show of seeking her out."

Her voice was even, but he could almost read her thoughts and knew that she was attempting to mask her hurt. He had never felt more like an unfeeling cad. Sneaking moments with her in the dead of night to take his pleasure with her while openly courting another. In that moment it didn't matter that she knew his true feelings and motives.

"Catherine—"

"Don't." The smile that she aimed at him was brittle. "I understand, truly. And you needn't fear. I will wait for you."

It spoke to her true generosity of spirit that she would try to give him a measure of comfort when she herself was hurting.

"I don't deserve you," he said as the carriage slowed to a halt.

She reached across and placed a hand on his thigh and his body, still hard with frustrated desire, leapt to life. "Perhaps not, but you have me at any rate."

The door started to open and she snatched back her hand. As he watched her descend from the carriage with the aid of a footman, a sense of panic settled over him. He wanted to call her back, but of course he didn't. He'd never counted himself a superstitious man, but in that moment he feared they were both tempting the fates.

CHAPTER TWELVE

CATHERINE STUDIED THE sketch she'd just completed and sighed. This was her third attempt at designing a new garden for the Worthingtons' town house, and she still wasn't happy with the results. The layout was nice and the plants she'd chosen were pretty, but overall it was ordinary. Perhaps if she introduced a couple of the plants she'd seen during her outing to Kew Gardens… She sighed again, louder. She couldn't indulge in that desire. Rose had mentioned that their gardener was older and wouldn't know how to care for plants that needed special provisions. Would he even bother to dig up the plants that needed to be housed indoors during the cold British winters, or would they be left to die? That uncertainty meant Catherine could only include plants in the design that were hardier. The same plants that were in every other garden in London.

Frustrated, she set the sketch aside and reached for a new piece of paper. Her hand stilled when, out of the corner of her eye, she saw movement. She looked up to see her sister standing in the library's doorway.

"I wondered where you'd disappeared to," Louisa said as she entered the room.

Catherine waved a hand over the papers that were spread out over the small desk at which she sat. "I find the morning light in here excellent for drawing."

Her sister approached and looked down at the various sketches. Her eyes settled on the one Catherine had drawn first.

"I don't remember the Worthingtons' garden being this large. Of course, I only glimpsed it through the garden doors during their musicale."

"I might have gotten carried away with that one," Catherine said as she moved that page off to the side and handed Louisa the three sketches she'd drawn for Rose. "These are what I've drawn for the Worthingtons."

Catherine didn't tell her sister that she'd been daydreaming about her perfect garden when she'd worked on that first drawing. It was filled with exotic plants that were completely impractical for the British climate, but with some careful planning and a little extra work, she believed she could achieve a setting that was truly out of the ordinary. She couldn't give voice to her desire to see that garden come to life on Kerrick's estate. Like a wish you guarded in your heart after seeing a falling star, she was afraid that to speak it aloud would doom it.

Louisa examined each sketch, shaking her head in wonder. "These are very good. I shouldn't be surprised. I've always admired your skill at drawing, and I think there are few who could rival your interest in gardens and plants. Still, I never imagined you would be able to design something this good."

Catherine leaned back in her chair. "It's more difficult than I imagined to bring to life something unique when the space is so limited."

"Perhaps so, but you've made a wonderful start here. I think the Worthingtons will find it hard to choose a favorite."

Catherine accepted the drawings back from her sister and set them aside. She wouldn't show them to Rose until she was happy with them. Something was missing, but she would have to think about it later. Right now she could only think about Louisa, who was looking fragile.

Catherine stood and, taking her sister's hand, led her to the window seat. "You look tired," she said. "Did you not sleep well last night?"

Louisa sat with a grimace. "I've been told the fatigue I'm feeling is normal and that it will pass at some point. I'm not convinced the doctor is telling me the truth."

"We'll stay home tonight." Catherine felt a pang of regret knowing she'd be giving up an opportunity to see Kerrick if they stayed in that evening, but at the same time it was a relief to know that for one night she wouldn't have to pretend he was nothing more than a family friend if their paths crossed.

"No." Louisa gave her head a firm shake. "I was just heading upstairs to have a nap. I'm sure I'll be more rested tonight."

"I don't mind," Catherine said. "To be honest, I'd enjoy a quiet evening. Life is so different in town than what we are used to."

"I should insist, but I do agree with you. It is something of a shock after the quiet life we used to lead."

"John would have hated it," Catherine said.

"John would have been away at school if he hadn't enlisted, not attending balls."

Seeing her sister's heartache, Catherine reached for

her hand and gave it a squeeze. "He doesn't hate you."

"You can't say that with certainty."

"I can." She hesitated a moment before deciding to tell her sister about that last conversation she'd had with their brother. "We argued during the ball Nicholas's grandmother hosted after you were married. He talked about leaving—"

"And you didn't tell me?"

"I couldn't. It was your wedding day... I never imagined he'd leave that night."

Louisa looked away and Catherine could see she still blamed herself.

"He didn't support your marriage, but John was there that night because he loves you. He could have left before the wedding, but he stayed. I still don't know why he felt he had to leave."

Louisa was silent for a moment. "I'm scared we'll never see him again." Her hand went to her belly, which was still flat. "That he'll never meet his niece or nephew and will never learn how happy Nicholas and I are."

Catherine wanted nothing more than to tell her sister that her fears were groundless, but she couldn't. Young men were dying every day in England's war with France. Instead, she pulled her sister into a heartfelt embrace.

She drew back when a soft knock sounded at the library door. Glad for the interruption, Catherine looked up to see a footman standing in the doorway. He held a small silver tray, upon which a note rested. He announced that a message had arrived for Catherine and her heart rate increased.

The footman approached and Catherine reached for the sealed note on the tray.

"Is it from Rose?" Louisa asked.

Catherine waited for the footman to leave before glancing down at where her name was inscribed on the heavy paper. She didn't recognize the handwriting.

"No," she said, her mind racing as she wondered if Kerrick had sent it.

"Are you going to open it?"

She hesitated for a moment but knew she couldn't hide the note's contents from her sister. Doing so would only arouse Louisa's suspicion that Catherine was keeping secrets. Telling herself that Kerrick wouldn't risk sending her a note that anyone could have intercepted, she turned over the note and broke the wax seal.

She unfolded the paper and glanced first at the signature at the bottom. She couldn't hold back the little stab of disappointment when she didn't see Kerrick's name. Calling herself a fool, she read the note.

"Who is it from?" Louisa was leaning forward in her seat, her eyes gleaming with curiosity.

"It's from Lord Thornton. He's invited me to a drive in Hyde Park this afternoon."

"That sounds lovely. Lord Thornton seems like such a nice young man." Louisa must have seen her hesitation because she added, "And if you go, I needn't feel so guilty about staying in tonight."

Catherine knew Louisa was only pushing her toward Thornton because she worried about her attachment to Kerrick. Still, she found herself having to bite her lip so as not to give voice to her annoyance.

"Will you accept?"

Catherine was on the verge of saying no, but then she remembered Kerrick's parting words to her the night before. He needed Lord Worthington to believe his interest in Rose was genuine, and he planned to take Rose out for a drive today. Would it not aid society's belief that she and Kerrick were merely friends if she was seen with Lord Thornton? Surely Kerrick would approve of her plan.

Convinced she was pursing the wisest course of action, the smile she gave her sister was genuine. "I think you're right. A bit of fresh air this afternoon would be just the thing."

IT WAS ALMOST ridiculous how many times she changed her clothing in a day. Before her sister married, the three Evans siblings—Catherine, Louisa, and their brother John—had lived in a modest cottage and on an even more modest income. They hadn't even been able to afford to hire a servant. And the dress Catherine chose to wear each morning was the one she still wore when she retired at night.

But all that had changed after a chance encounter with the new Marquess of Overlea, then considered to be an enemy of the family since it was Nicholas's uncle who had been responsible for robbing their family of their home and land. Catherine had been stunned when, mere days later, Louisa had accepted Nicholas's proposal of marriage.

Now their entire life was different. Aside from their brother, who had chosen to join the fight against Napoleon rather than accept anything from Overlea's family, they had gone from poverty to the complete opposite. And so quickly that Catherine still found it difficult to remember, at times, that she no longer had to worry about anything. Well, anything aside from the matter of finding a husband. She sincerely hoped that issue would soon be resolved and that she and Kerrick could make public their courtship.

But until that time arrived, she would have to pay attention to the man seated beside her in the curricle. Lord Thornton seemed in especially high spirits that afternoon. Catherine liked him, she really did, but he reminded her so much of her brother. Yes, he was a few years older than John, who was now nineteen years of age, but like her brother, Thornton was fair. And he seemed so young. Especially when compared to Kerrick.

She blushed when she realized that Lord Thornton had asked her a question while she'd been thinking about another man.

"I'm sorry," she said. "I was just thinking about last night."

His smile reminded her of an overeager puppy. "I'm so glad that I thought to attend the Hastings' rout. I almost didn't and I would have hated to miss seeing you."

"I do like the intimacy of the smaller house parties."

"I was disappointed you had to leave so early. I was wondering..." Thornton swallowed. "Perhaps at the next ball I could partner with you more than once."

For a moment she actually considered granting his request. Dancing several times with Viscount Thornton would signal that he was a serious contender for her hand in matrimony. It would definitely go a long way toward ensuring that her name wouldn't be romantically linked to Kerrick's. But in the end, she didn't feel comfortable sending that message to Thornton or to society.

"It is still a little early in the season for such declarations, is it not?"

His expression earnest, he replied, "I don't believe in waiting when I see something I want."

She was at a loss as to how to reply and it occurred to her that Rose would know exactly what to say. Catherine had next to no experience with romance beyond what she and Kerrick had shared. She lacked the ability to set a man down with the finesse Rose possessed. Her friend would have said something witty and had Lord Thornton believing he still had a chance even while she was putting him off.

As if thinking about her friend had conjured her, another carriage pulled up next to theirs on the crowded Hyde Park bridle path. Relief at the timely interruption went through her when she saw it was occupied with Kerrick and Rose.

"What a happy coincidence to run into you here," Rose called across the two men who separated them. "Perhaps we can walk for a bit?"

Kerrick's expression was neutral, but the slight tightening of his jaw told her that he was not happy to see her there. A quick glance at Thornton, who appeared happy at Rose's suggestion, indicated that he hadn't noticed Kerrick's displeasure. Catherine saw no reason to disagree. Being seen in public with different companions would help further the perception that he was nothing more than a family friend.

The carriages were pulled to the side and Thornton handed her down. When he held on to her hand for several seconds longer than necessary, she couldn't stop herself from glancing at Kerrick. He wasn't looking at them, but the stiff set of his shoulders was proof that he'd noticed the intimate gesture and that he did not approve.

"Try not to wander off and cause a panic," Rose said with mock censure after reaching her side.

Catherine could only shake her head in chagrin. "You heard about that?"

Rose laughed, the sound light and musical. "With the number of men involved in the search party, I don't think there's anyone who hasn't heard the story."

Her eyes met Kerrick's. He hadn't been in town yet for that embarrassing incident, but she'd told him about it that first night when he'd danced with her.

Pulling her gaze from his, she turned back to Rose and said with a small wince, "I was afraid that would be the case."

Rose drew an arm through hers and proceeded to stroll away from the carriages at a moderate pace, the men walking alongside them. "After hearing the story, I realized that I must get to know you. I decided that anyone who could have half the eligible men of the *ton* chasing after her was someone I had to meet."

Catherine felt a twinge of alarm at the implication in her friend's statement. "You make it sound like the incident was calculated. I assure you it wasn't."

"At the time I thought it was," Rose said with a shrug. "But fear not—now that I have come to know you, I realize that you truly had wandered off to look at some plants."

"In my defense, I was newly arrived in London and as it was my first time in Hyde Park. I was curious."

Kerrick added, "When I stayed at Overlea Manor last autumn, she was almost always in the conservatory. Overlea's grandmother is rather fond of unusual plants, and Catherine made it her mission to try to catalog them all."

"I'm not surprised to hear it," Rose said. The twinkle in her eye gave Catherine only a second of warning that her friend was up to something before she turned to Lord Thornton. "And you, my lord? Do you share Miss Evans's love of plants?"

The look on Thornton's face made it seem as

though Rose had just asked him if the sky was purple. Catherine frowned and he rushed to reply. "I admit that I've never paid much attention to them. My mother says that when I was younger I was often to be found tearing up the garden with my brothers. After that, I spent most of my time away at school."

Catherine laughed. "My brother John was much the same way. I fear most boys are just too full of energy to sit back and enjoy the beauty of nature."

"I never asked," Kerrick said. "Did you finish cataloging all the plants? I confess I couldn't tell a plant commonly found in England from the more exotic ones."

"There are still a few I haven't been able to discover in any of the plant texts in the library at Overlea Manor. I've already purchased a few books I plan to take back with me when the season is over." She sighed, adding, "I wish I'd thought to bring sketches of the plants with me to London. Mr. Clifton might have been able to tell me what they were."

"Clifton? Who is that?" Thornton asked.

"The head gardener at Kew Gardens."

"Lord Kerrick arranged to take Miss Evans on a tour of the gardens there." With a sly glance in Catherine's direction, Rose added, "It must have been very romantic."

Thornton frowned and Catherine could have throttled her friend. It was clear Rose was wasting no time in trying to play matchmaker between her and Kerrick. She squeezed her friend's arm in silent entreaty that she desist and turned to Lord Thornton. "Of course it wasn't. The Duke and Duchess of Clarington were also present during the tour."

Thornton seemed satisfied with her answer. "Perhaps the next time you are in London I will be in a position to take you to Kew Gardens myself so you can show the sketches of your mystery plants to this Mr. Clifton."

Thornton's expression was so earnest that Catherine felt a pang of remorse for falsely raising his hopes. A quick glance at Kerrick showed him to be studiously avoiding eye contact with her. She was about to change the subject rather than reply when she saw the telltale tightening of his jaw. A thrill went through her at the small proof of his jealousy. A spark of mischief goaded her to test her theory.

"Perhaps you will," she said, meeting his gaze and then looking down in an attempt at coyness.

She'd copied the action from Rose, who used it to great effect. It appeared to work, because when she looked at Thornton out of the corner of her eye, his grin had broadened. It took her a moment to realize that Kerrick had stopped walking. She'd been so wrapped up in her little deception that she hadn't noticed. Rose, however, had and she pulled at Catherine's arm, bringing her to a halt. The glare in her friend's eyes spoke volumes. Rose was annoyed at her for flirting with the wrong man.

Kerrick offered Rose his arm, and with one last look that signaled Catherine would be hearing about her attempt to thwart her matchmaking, Rose took it. Their promenade at an end, Catherine was left to take Thornton's arm as they returned to the carriages. Rose and Kerrick walked a few steps ahead of them. Kerrick bent to murmur something for Rose's ears only, and Catherine had to clench her teeth as her friend laughed gaily.

The two of them are only acting a part, she told herself. But that didn't stop her from feeling a pang of jealousy herself when Kerrick helped Rose into his carriage. She wanted so much to be the woman who got to sit beside him in public. They'd had a wonderful encounter the previous evening in his closed carriage, but in the clear light of day that was no longer enough.

CHAPTER THIRTEEN

IT HAD BEEN almost a week since she'd last seen Kerrick, and Catherine felt his absence keenly. If he thought to punish her for flirting with Viscount Thornton, he'd succeeded. Each night after returning home from one of the many evening entertainments, she had to battle back the temptation to sneak out and return to Kerrick's town house. She'd promised him that she wouldn't make a repeat visit, but as she lay in bed imagining all the delightfully wicked things they had done together, longing for his touch, her resolve weakened.

It didn't help that their brief interlude in the Duke

of Clarington's carriage had shown her that pleasure between a man and a woman was not limited to the bedroom. She found herself looking for Kerrick each evening. Imagined him whisking her away to a private room—she wasn't particular, even a closet would do—and making love to her again. And each night, when he failed to show, she returned home more frustrated than ever with the current state of their relationship.

But more important than her desire for Kerrick was her resolve that he not see her as a foolish girl who would allow her selfish wants to place his current mission in jeopardy. Logically she knew that he trusted her—he wouldn't have confided in her if he didn't. But when she was alone at night she remembered how close he and Louisa had been when he'd stayed at Overlea Manor after her sister's wedding to Nicholas. A small part of her still wondered if he saw her as a substitute for Louisa. She was able to push those thoughts away in the clear light of day, but as the days passed and she failed to see him, her doubt began to grow.

She needed to see him again, so it was an immense relief to learn that he would be present at the small dinner party Louisa and Nicholas were holding that evening. She'd known he was invited but had feared he would send his regrets yet again.

Remembering Kerrick's reaction the last time she'd

worn her yellow evening gown to the theater, she suffered a moment of uncertainty when she told her maid she wanted to wear the more modest light green gown—the one she'd worn the night she'd visited his town house. The night they'd made love. Most men wouldn't remember that, but she knew Kerrick would. He always noticed the smallest of details, a trait which she suspected was invaluable to him in his work for the government.

Her sister's and brother-in-law's muted voices in the hallway as they passed her bedroom told her it was time for dinner. Taking a deep breath, she smoothed her hands over her gown and glanced into the mirror above her dressing table to ensure she looked her best. Six days had passed since that outing to Hyde Park… seven since she and Kerrick had been alone in his carriage. She shouldn't be nervous at the thought of seeing him again, but she was.

She hesitated at the top of the stairs when a knock sounded at the front door. A moment later, she heard the Duke of Clarington's voice and she had to shake her head at her own nonsense. She was making too much of Kerrick's absence.

She'd just reached the bottom of the stairs when there was another knock at the front door. She waited, butterflies taking flight in her belly, while the butler opened the door. When she saw Kerrick standing on the landing, she couldn't stop the smile that spread across her face. As he stepped over the threshold, his gazed locked on hers for a moment before moving down. When his eyes met hers again, there was a heat there that told her he was remembering the last time he'd seen her in that dress—and what had followed. The weight of that gaze was almost a physical caress.

She waited while Kerrick handed his hat and gloves to the butler and approached her. He offered her his arm with a slightly raised brow, and to her mortification she blushed. Aware of the other man still standing behind them, she took his arm without a word. They were only steps away from the drawing room and could hear the voices of the others, but neither moved to join them. Clearly sensing that he was *de trop*, the butler removed himself after offering a slight bow in their direction.

"You look worried," Kerrick said when they were alone. "Is anything the matter?"

Catherine shook her head. "Not anymore."

He squeezed her hand where it rested on his arm and was about to say something more when Louisa stepped into the hallway. Her expression made it clear that she wasn't happy to find them alone together. Louisa already knew about Catherine's feelings for

Kerrick, but it was important that she not suspect there was now something more between them.

"I thought perhaps something was amiss since you hadn't joined us."

It was with reluctance that Catherine stepped away from him. "I was checking to make sure this man was, indeed, Lord Kerrick," she said, aiming for levity. "It's been so long since we've seen him, I couldn't be certain."

"I apologize for my absence," Kerrick said. "I am not used to attending quite so many balls, and I'm afraid I needed a bit of a respite from all the various entertainments."

"I'm sure we must all be such a trial to you," Louisa said. "Nicholas told me he's already been to more plays and balls this season than he's attended in all his previous years put together."

"I'll admit it's a little lonely now that my closest friends have traded their usual ways for marital bliss. If I want to see them, I'm forced to attend those balls myself and give up my bachelor haunts."

"Poor Kerrick," Louisa said with a fond smile.

Catherine had to grit her teeth and force back her misgivings when she saw the evidence in Kerrick's face of the affection he bore her sister. More than that, she hated that she still wondered just how far that affection went. But at least the tension that had arisen from being found whispering together in the hallway had dissipated, and together they joined Nicholas and the Claringtons in the drawing room.

Dinner was more difficult than she could have imagined. Their party was small, so there was no chance to engage Kerrick in private conversation. He sat across from her, but Louisa was between them at the foot of the table. Every word they spoke was, naturally, heard by her sister. The meal seemed to drag on forever, but Catherine told herself that surely she and Kerrick would be able to manage a conversation away from the others later in the evening.

When dinner was over and the men joined the women in the drawing room after staying behind to have their port, Catherine looked up eagerly. Kerrick's gaze met hers and in it she saw something that made her pulse leap. He started to move toward her but was interrupted when Louisa stepped between them and captured his attention.

It didn't take her long to realize that her sister was going to great lengths to ensure that she and Kerrick wouldn't have the opportunity for even a moment of private conversation. She wanted to scream with frustration every time she turned around to find Louisa watching her, and whenever Kerrick approached her, or she him, her sister made a point of intercepting them.

"What are you doing?" she hissed to Louisa after dragging her into a corner of the room.

"I'm protecting you from yourself." The stiff set of Louisa's shoulders indicated that she was bracing herself for Catherine's angry response.

She wasn't sure how to reply. She understood the motivation behind her sister's actions and was torn between frustration that Louisa still treated her like a child and sadness that her relationship with Kerrick must remain a secret. She was saved from having to answer, however, when Nicholas joined them. From his curious expression, it was clear he'd witnessed their exchange. It took every ounce of strength she possessed to turn and smile at her brother-in-law.

"I hope you aren't overtiring yourself," he said to Louisa, concern etched along his features.

The smile Louisa gave her husband contained more than a hint of indulgence. "Stop worrying, I am fine."

Catherine couldn't help but see the irony in her sister's statement and was tempted to echo the words back to her with respect to Louisa's concern about her feelings for Kerrick. She opened her mouth to do just that, but was interrupted when the duchess joined them.

"Miss Evans," she said, tucking her hand around Catherine's arm. "Lord Kerrick just told me that you are designing a new garden for the Worthingtons."

"Yes, I am." She ignored the look of concern that passed between Louisa and Nicholas.

"After our outing to Kew Gardens, I must confess that I am inspired to expand the gardens at our estate." The duchess paused for a moment before adding, "I don't suppose you have any drawings of your plans? I was very impressed with your knowledge and am more than a little curious to see them."

"I do have a few sketches, but I admit I'm not quite happy with them. I fear I am no Capability Brown."

"I'm sure you are being modest. Would it be too much of an imposition to ask to see them?"

Catherine didn't miss the gleam in the other woman's eyes and suspected she did not merely wish to discuss gardens with her. Like Rose, and unlike her sister, she knew that the duchess hoped to facilitate a match between her and Kerrick. There was no other reason why she would have convinced her husband to help set up that private meeting in the carriage.

"They're in the library. Did you want to see them now?"

"If you don't mind," the duchess said with a smile that seemed far too innocent.

Not waiting for her reply, she all but whisked Catherine from the room. As they made their way to the library, Catherine braced herself for the questions she knew were coming.

She didn't have to wait long. After crossing the threshold, the duchess closed the door and turned to face her.

"How are things progressing between you and Lord Kerrick?"

Catherine walked over to the small desk where she kept the drawings she was working on. Her back to the duchess as she reached for the small stack of papers, she said, "We are friends."

The duchess sighed. "I'd hoped that after your meeting in the carriage the two of you would have moved beyond friendship."

Catherine turned to face her, the drawings clutched to her chest, and voiced the question that had been worrying her. "Do you think His Grace will tell Nicholas about that evening?"

"Not if he wishes to keep his head. I don't think Overlea would be happy to learn that he helped to arrange a private meeting between his best friend and his young sister-in-law. He's quite protective of you."

Catherine released the breath she'd been holding. "I know. I hate to think how protective he'll be if Louisa has a girl."

The duchess eyed her closely. "Rumors are circulating… Kerrick is expected to ask for Rose Hardwick's hand in marriage any day now."

Catherine had to force herself not to look away when she replied. "I'm afraid those rumors might be true."

"How can you be so calm? If that is true, then he has treated you abominably."

Unable to hold the woman's gaze, she looked away. She didn't have to feign her emotions when she said, "I won't lie and say the thought of he and Rose marrying leaves me feeling more than a little ill. You know I care for him, as does my sister. In fact, I fear the entire world knows it." She winced and rushed to add, "But Lord Kerrick has not behaved inappropriately."

To keep the duchess from questioning her further, Catherine knew she was going to have to lie outright. "I fear Kerrick sees me only as Louisa's little sister. He wants to do something nice for her and Nicholas after the baby is born. That's why he wanted to speak to me in private—so no one would learn about his plans."

It was clear the duchess didn't believe her. "And what is it he's planning?"

"I can't betray his confidence. You'll have to learn of it when the others do."

The duchess seemed to consider her words for a moment before speaking. "Perhaps I can help."

Catherine closed her eyes for a moment, not bothering to hide her frustration. It would seem that the entire world was aligned together in throwing obstacles in the way of Kerrick's investigation. She couldn't blame the duchess, however. How could she know that the only way for her and Kerrick to be together was to allow him to continue to grow closer to another woman?

"I wish you wouldn't," she said, meeting the duchess's concerned gaze head-on. "I know your heart is in the right place, and I do thank you, but this entire situation is already more than a little difficult for me."

Catherine could tell the duchess didn't want to let the matter drop, but instead she reached for the drawings that Catherine still held clutched to her chest. Relieved, Catherine handed them to the other woman.

The remainder of the evening passed quickly. When she and the duchess returned to the drawing room, Louisa was playing at the pianoforte and the men were discussing some new horseflesh they'd seen at Tattersall's. Catherine made a mental note to let Kerrick know that he had to plan something special for the arrival of Louisa and Nicholas's first child so the duchess wouldn't know she'd been lied to.

She questioned whether she'd ever have that opportunity. When she retired for the evening, she was beyond frustrated. She'd spent the entire evening in Kerrick's company, but the only private exchange they'd had was after his arrival when they'd shared a few words.

Catherine mulled over her situation as her maid helped her out of her dress and into her nightgown. So engrossed was she in her own thoughts that it wasn't until she was seated at her dressing table that she noticed her maid was strangely silent. Normally Lily liked to chatter, but she hadn't said a word as she removed the pins from Catherine's hair.

She turned in her seat to face the young woman. "You are very quiet this evening, Lily."

Her maid looked away and seemed to wrestle with herself before speaking. "I'm so sorry, Miss Evans."

Guilt flickered over the other woman's face and the breath froze in Catherine's lungs as her mind leapt to the worst possible scenario. "Who did you tell?" she finally managed.

Lily appeared confused. "Tell?"

"About my visit to Lord Kerrick's town house. Who did you tell?"

Her maid shook her head vehemently. "Oh no, I didn't tell anyone. I promised not to."

The tightness in her chest eased a bit. "Then what are you sorry for, Lily?"

The woman hesitated a moment before reaching into the pocket of her uniform and pulling out a folded note. "The footman gave me this note to give to you. He said it was from Her Grace, but the handwriting seemed like it was written by a man. I wasn't sure if I should give it to you."

It was clear her maid was having some misgivings about agreeing to keep her mistress's secrets. Catherine kept her tone even when she replied. "Do you trust me to know what I am doing?"

That was the crux of the matter. Did Lily see her as a flighty young girl acting impetuously, chasing after a man who was unavailable?

"If Lady Overlea finds out—"

"Nothing will happen to you, Lily. My sister knows me well enough to know that I can be very stubborn when it comes to getting what I want. If she learns of my... activities... and blames anyone, it will be me. I'll make sure that nothing happens to you."

"And what about you, Miss Catherine? Who will make sure that nothing happens to you?"

Catherine held her hand out for the note. When Lily released her tight hold on it, she smiled at the young woman. "I will. You and I both know that Lord

Kerrick would do nothing to anger Lord Overlea."

That wasn't strictly the truth, but the words seemed to give Lily some comfort. Catherine ached to dismiss her and read the note, but if she expected her maid to believe she was a capable young woman with a good head on her shoulders, she was going to have to act the part—no matter how much it killed her to wait.

Catherine turned back to the mirror, placed the note on her dressing table, and waited for her maid to finish taking down her hair and brushing it out. Finally, after what seemed an eternity, Catherine bade the woman good night and watched her leave the room.

Her hands were almost shaking when she turned the note over. It was sealed and across the front her name was written in a bold scrawl. Catherine broke the seal and unfolded the paper. Her eyes eagerly scanned the few words that were written there.

I am doing all that I can to conclude the matter we discussed. Please do not give up hope.

I miss you.

—K

Catherine clutched the note to her chest. It was a poor substitute for Kerrick's presence, but it was all she had of him.

CATHERINE SLEPT LATER than normal the following morning. Since her sister's pregnancy meant that Louisa had difficulty keeping food down in the morning, and since Nicholas tended to hover over his wife most mornings, they rarely went downstairs for breakfast. Catherine had, therefore, started asking for a breakfast tray to be brought to her room. She rang for her maid to bring up her customary tea and toast, but when the young woman arrived she informed Catherine that Rose had called was waiting for her in the drawing room.

Lily helped her dress quickly while Catherine tried to remember if she'd made plans to go shopping with Rose that morning. She'd had so much on her mind of late that she wouldn't be surprised to learn she'd forgotten.

When she entered the drawing room ten minutes later, she could tell immediately that Rose was upset. She sat perched on the edge of the settee, her hands clenched in her lap as she stared off into space.

Catherine crossed the room and sat next to her friend. "I thought that perhaps I had forgotten another one of your excursions to Bond Street, but from the look on your face I can see that isn't the case. I'm almost afraid to ask what has happened."

Rose glanced to the doorway to make sure they were alone before replying. "My parents think I have an early appointment with the dressmaker and don't know I've come to see you."

"I assume you led them to believe that, but I don't understand why."

"It's simply dreadful, Catherine. Apparently Father has been hearing rumors about Lord Kerrick spending so much time here."

Rose's concern confused her. "It is hardly a secret that he and my brother-in-law are the best of friends. Everyone knows that. Why should it matter if he occasionally has dinner here?"

"It's because of you. Father thinks that Kerrick is playing me for a fool and that it is you he means to marry."

Catherine turned away and shook her head as she struggled to hide the panic that was beginning to rise at her friend's words.

"You already know how I feel," Rose said when Catherine didn't reply. "I hope fervently that what he says is true. But Father is very angry about it and he has forbidden me from seeing you again. If you can imagine, he believes you are using me to get closer to Lord Kerrick. I fear he would never forgive me if he learned that I am doing everything in my power to promote the match."

"You shouldn't say such a thing—"

"Whyever not? I've seen the way he looks at you, and it is clear I am not the only person who has noticed."

Catherine felt as though she were being ripped in two. She hated lying to her friend, especially since it was clear that Rose was no fool and could see for herself how she and Kerrick felt despite their attempts to hide it. That others were beginning to notice was a disaster. The very last thing she wanted was to betray Kerrick's trust in her. She couldn't be the reason his inquiries failed or he would never again trust her. And if she lost his trust, would he continue to care for her?

She wanted to believe he loved her as much as she did him, but she couldn't quiet that niggling voice that told her she could be easily replaced. Kerrick was by no means an old man—he was only nine-and-twenty—but he was more experienced than she. He was a man of the world and she knew he'd had lovers. How realistic would it be to believe he wouldn't be able to replace her in a heartbeat?

She had to choose her words carefully or her very

perceptive friend would know she was lying.

"Kerrick and I are just friends."

Rose shook her head in exasperation. "Are you trying to convince me or yourself? Lord Kerrick and I are not yet betrothed. If you would exert yourself a little, allow him to see how you truly feel about him, I know in my heart that he would give up his ridiculous courtship of me. I don't understand why you don't at least try."

"I am afraid, Rose. Afraid that my feelings for Kerrick will only end in heartbreak." And that, at its core, was the earth-shattering truth. The one she tried not to think about as she struggled to push away her doubts.

"I think my father means to press him to declare his intentions soon."

A stab of panic went through Catherine. "Would he really do that?

Rose nodded solemnly. "I believe so. I know he's always desired a match between us—Mama is very good friends with his mother and when I was young they often talked about how wonderful it would be to unite our families. But lately it's not just a wish. He seems almost desperate for a match between us."

Catherine hadn't wanted to believe that Lord Worthington had committed whatever crime it was that Kerrick was investigating, but Rose's confusion about her father's unusual behavior was setting off internal alarm bells.

She tried to keep her voice even as she asked, "Is there a reason for this change?"

"Not that I can think of," Rose said with a small shake of her head. "Hoping to ease the way for you and Kerrick, I told Father that I didn't want to marry him."

Catherine winced inwardly as she imagined how Kerrick would react to that news. "What did he say to that?"

"He wouldn't hear of it. He told me that I had to make sure to hold Lord Kerrick's favor. But worse than the fact that my father doesn't care if I have any feelings for my future husband was the look in his eyes. I was going to press the issue, but something in Father's eyes frightened me. He looked afraid."

"Of what?" Catherine asked, finding that she had to work to keep her breathing even.

"I don't know. We aren't having money problems… We were until recently, but Father came into some sort of inheritance. And let us be frank—I could align myself with any number of men, some with titles much more prestigious and estates far wealthier than Lord Kerrick's."

"But not the man you really want."

"No," Rose said, and Catherine could see that she was trying to put on a brave face. "He might as well be a figment of my imagination for how likely I am to be noticed by him. I daresay I'll forget about him in time. He's far too old for me anyway."

Catherine's curiosity was piqued, but from Rose's closed expression she knew her friend had no intention of sharing anything further about the mysterious man. It was only then that Catherine realized just how stressful this situation was on her friend as well. She'd been so wrapped up in her own worries that she hadn't fully given thought to the pressure Rose was facing. And if her father was guilty of any wrongdoing, the repercussions she faced would likely lead to her ruin. Just thinking about it threatened to make her breathless with dread.

"I'm not sure what I can say or do that would make this whole situation easier," Catherine said.

"There's nothing you can do. I just wanted to let you know that I won't be allowed see you for a little while. And if Lord Kerrick does propose and I deny him…" A shudder went through her. "To be honest, I'm not sure Father would actually allow me to do so. One way or another, this situation must come to an end soon."

Rose stood and Catherine followed her to the door.

After saying their good-byes, she returned to her bedroom to pen a note to Lord Kerrick. She had to warn him about what was coming with Lord Worthington, but she also had to be careful about how she worded the note lest someone else see it. In the end, she decided the situation was urgent enough to warrant her use of the code they had devised that would tell him she needed to see him right away. Impatient, she took a sheet of paper from her small lap desk, dipped her quill in a bottle of ink, and wrote one word—*Daffodils*.

CHAPTER FOURTEEN

CATHERINE KNEW KERRICK wasn't fond of opera, but still she looked for him that evening. When she didn't see him before the curtain rose, she was on tenterhooks during the performance, hoping that he would drop by their box during the intermission. Or perhaps waylay them after the opera was over.

When he failed to show, she began to second-guess herself. Kerrick had assured her that he would find a way to speak to her if she sent him a note with their code word. But it was impossible not to worry when she wondered if Lord Worthington was, even at that moment, pressing Kerrick to declare his intentions to

Rose. If Kerrick was forced to do so for the sake of his investigation and if Rose was pressured by her parents to accept... then it was all over. She knew Kerrick enough to know he had a deeply ingrained sense of honor. Even if society did not frown heavily on a gentleman for behaving in such a selfish manner, she knew he would never humiliate Rose by breaking off an engagement.

By the time they returned to the town house, her concern had grown into a huge ball of despair that weighed heavily on her heart. She wasn't successful in hiding her feelings. But when Nicholas asked her what was the matter, she managed a small smile and told him that her head was aching.

She made her way up to her bedroom and found her maid approaching from the other end of the hallway.

"You don't look well, Miss Evans," Lily said as they entered the bedroom together.

"It's just a touch of the headache. I'm sure I'll be fine after a good night's sleep."

Lily took down her hair with quick, efficient motions. "Would you like me to bring you something before you turn in?"

"That won't be necessary," she said, standing so her maid could undo the buttons at the back of her gown.

She barely managed to hold back a small squeak of

surprise when she caught a quick movement behind the dressing screen in the corner of her room. Her heart gave a small leap and she kept her eyes trained in that direction as Lily helped her out of her dress and the constraining corset she wore beneath. When her maid moved to the bed to fetch her nightgown, her back to the screen, Kerrick popped his head out from behind it. He raised a finger to his lips to signal that she should remain silent and gave her a quick wink before ducking back behind the screen. Catherine didn't realize she'd been grinning until her maid commented on it.

"You seem to be in a better mood already."

Catherine nodded and did her best to school her expression. "It is such a relief to be able to take a deep breath again," she said before ushering Lily to the door.

"But your nightgown..."

"I am so tired I think I'll just sleep in my chemise."

When Lily left, Catherine locked the door behind her and offered up a quick thank-you that several rooms stood between her bedroom and the master bedroom. When she turned to face the screen, Kerrick had already moved into the open.

Her voice was barely above a whisper when she asked, "How did you get in here?" She shook her head, amazed that he would risk being caught sneaking into her bedroom and, if truth be told, more than a little delighted at his audacity.

"I've been a guest here more than once over the years. I know this house almost as well as I do my own."

"How did you know which room was mine?"

His gaze swept over her, dark and intent, and she became aware that the material of her chemise was so fine as to be almost transparent. "It wasn't difficult… it smells just like you."

Her heart melted and for a moment she forgot the real reason for his visit. His next words were like a splash of cold water, dousing her romanticism.

"You sent me a note with our code word."

"My maid is nervous about our communication—it was necessary to make her believe our correspondence was about something innocent." She had to force her gaze away and try to regain her composure before she could continue. "Have you seen Lord Worthington today?"

He shook his head. "After receiving your note, I thought it wise to hear what you had to say first."

Relief washed over her. It wasn't too late. Kerrick hadn't been pressured yet into making an offer of marriage.

"Rose visited me this morning and was quite distraught. Apparently her father is under the impression that I am using her to get closer to you and that you aren't serious about her. He plans to demand that you make your intentions toward Rose public as soon as possible."

Kerrick swore softly and lowered himself onto the edge of her bed. When he dropped his head into his hands, she sat next to him.

"I thought I should warn you."

He nodded but remained silent for several long moments.

"What are you going to do?" Catherine asked.

Kerrick lifted his head and turned to look at her. "I'm going to try to put him off since I have no intention of becoming formally betrothed to Rose. She seems lovely, but I draw the line at marrying someone for the sake of this inquiry. I couldn't, in good conscience, use her in such a manner and then cast her off when I was done."

"Rose cares deeply for someone else."

"I'm not surprised."

They both knew that Rose was intent on arranging a match between Kerrick and Catherine, but there was something in his simple statement that had her convinced Kerrick knew something she didn't.

"She won't tell me who, but I have a feeling you know."

"I have my suspicions, but that's all they are. And

no, I won't tell you who it is." He gave a rueful shake of his head when she blew out a breath of frustration.

"Rose said that she thought her father was scared, but she couldn't say why." She hesitated briefly before asking the question she didn't really want to know the answer to. "Do you think it's possible he's guilty of whatever crime he's suspected of doing?"

Kerrick seemed to weigh his words carefully. "It's beginning to look that way. More than that, I cannot say." He took hold of one of her hands and gripped it tightly. "After what you've told me, I'm going to have to be more careful to separate myself from you. That means I won't be accepting any further invitations to dine here, and I will do what I can to make sure we aren't seen together, even in public."

His words brought on an almost unbearable sadness. She tugged her hand from his and stood. "Is that why you came here tonight?" she asked, her heart constricting. "To tell me we can't see one another at all? That we can't even speak if our paths should cross in public?"

He closed the space between them and drew her into his arms. "No, I'm here because I can't stand the very thought of staying away from you."

His mouth descended on hers, but unlike his other kisses, which had held a hint of desperation, this one was slow, thorough, and utterly devastating. When he drew back slightly, she followed him, unwilling to end the kiss so quickly.

Half afraid that he was about to take his leave, she wrapped her arms around his neck and leaned into him. "I hate being separated from you," she whispered as he rained kisses down the side of her neck.

He lifted his head and stared down at her, his expression solemn. "We can't go on like this... I can't go on like this. One more week. Then, even if I haven't discovered any concrete proof one way or the other, I'm done."

His fervent words were punctuated by a sharp tug on her chemise. The delicate lawn fabric tore slightly and he stripped it away from her body.

Catherine's heart threatened to explode out of her chest as she reached to undo the buttons of his waistcoat. He stilled her action with a hand over hers.

"Not yet. My patience is almost at an end and I can't guarantee I'll be able to make this last once I feel your skin against mine."

"What if I don't want to wait?"

His jaw clenched, but instead of replying, he swung her into his arms and walked the few steps to the bed. Her naked body was held against his fully clothed one. She should have been embarrassed, but instead the difference in their states of undress, the way her skin slid against the fine wool of his coat and the silk of his waistcoat, heightened her awareness of the decadence of their actions.

He lowered her onto the bed and followed her down, shifting onto his side next to her. He ran a hand down her length, as though memorizing her shape, and she shivered.

"Have I ever mentioned that your perfume drives me insane? Exotic, like the flowers you enjoy so much, and not at all what one would expect from looking at you." He underscored his words by burying his face in the side of her neck and licking her there.

"I fear I am not at all like other demure maidens my age."

"Thank God for that," he said, taking her mouth again.

There was very little talking after that as he used his hands and mouth to worship her body. Finally, when she was ready to scream in frustration from the release he seemed determined to withhold from her, he thrust two fingers into her and used his thumb to stroke that place where all sensation seemed to center. He gazed down at her intently as he brought her to the very pinnacle, capturing her mouth just in time to swallow her cries of completion.

She watched in silence, floating between languor and anticipation of what was to come next, as Kerrick stood and began to undress. With each item of clothing he removed, her heart rate began to increase again. When he was down to his trousers, she could no longer remain still. She rose and placed her hand over the hard ridge of his arousal.

His arms fell to his side and he watched her intently as she undid the buttons of his fall. When the material fell open, she reached in and wrapped her hand around him. He groaned and began to lower his head to take her mouth again, but she stopped him by placing her other hand against his lips.

"It is now my turn, I believe," she said, loving the way his breath hitched when she placed her mouth over his chest.

She licked his flat nipple and his hard length leapt in her hand, telling her how much he liked it when she did that. So she licked him again as she stroked him.

"If you keep doing that, the evening will be coming to an end very quickly."

The strain in his voice underscored his words, but she didn't care. She loved being able to explore him the way he had explored her a few minutes before. Ignoring him, she dropped kisses down his abdomen. She released him to pull down his trousers. She remembered something she had overheard once and hesitated a moment before deciding that her desire to please him outweighed her shyness.

She lowered herself onto the edge of the bed and met his gaze. He was still standing, his erection level with her chin. She almost laughed at the expression on his face—a mixture of disbelief and hope. She took hold of him and ran her lips along his length before taking him into her mouth.

He swore but didn't move as she twirled her tongue against him. Remembering how he liked to have her move her hand along his length, she mimicked the action with her mouth, taking him deeper.

He shuddered, his hands tightening in her hair briefly before pulling her mouth away from him.

"Christ, Catherine, where in heaven's name did you learn to do that?"

She licked her lips and noticed the way his eyes followed the action. "I overheard two maids talking about it. I was scandalized at the time, but now I want nothing more than to take you into my mouth again and give you pleasure."

He closed his eyes briefly as though he were in pain before tumbling them both onto the bed. She thought he was going to roll her under him, but instead he rolled onto his back and lifted her over him. He spread her thighs so they rested on each side of his hips.

"That time will come, but it won't be tonight. Right now I need to be inside you."

He pressed her downward so that her intimate flesh pressed against the length of him. Now it was her turn to close her eyes as desire, hot and swift, swept through her.

"Ride me, Catherine," he said, shifting her so that his arousal was against her entrance. "Show me how much you want me."

She was powerless to do otherwise and allowed him to drag her down over him. He filled her to bursting and she had to bite her lower lip to keep from crying out with pleasure.

When she hesitated a moment, uncertain what to do next, his grip tightened on her hips.

"Like this," he said, raising her until only the tip of him was inside her, then slamming her down over him again.

She took over, shifting slightly so that each stroke brushed up against that bundle of nerves at the top of her slit. Kerrick released her hips and covered her breasts with his hands. When he pinched her nipples, she felt heat streak down to her core. She didn't resist when he pressed one hand against her back and brought her down so he could take one rosy-tipped peak into his mouth.

It was too much. The feel of his mouth drawing on her while he continued to play with her other breast. She lowered herself onto him once, twice more, then shattered. He released her then to grip her hips, and she was grateful because she no longer had the strength to continue. Instead, he held her while he stroked into her. Their eyes met and, remembering what had happened the last time they had made love, she steeled herself for that moment when he would lift her away from him. But instead, he brought her back down against him and closed his eyes while he found his release within her body.

She collapsed against his chest, ridiculously happy that he hadn't spent outside her body. That, more than any words he could have uttered, told her that he'd meant what he'd said. He planned to end his investigation and commit to her. Finally.

HE WAS A PORTRAIT of calm as he stood on the edge of the ballroom's dance floor, but inside, every nerve stood on edge, his very skin feeling too tight. It had taken an almost inhuman effort to tear himself away from Catherine last night, and he couldn't shake the feeling that something was about to go terribly wrong. He was being pressed upon from all sides. Brantford had definite expectations of him, expectations that played right into Worthington's hands. Rose also had expectations that he'd give up his courtship and save her from disappointing her father when she rejected him.

The only person who wasn't making demands of him was Catherine, and perversely, that fact annoyed him. He'd asked her to be patient while he completed this one last obligation to the Home Office, and it bothered him more than a little that she was doing just that. As his frustration with his fruitless and seemingly endless line of inquiry increased, so did his impatience with Catherine. It wasn't logical, but apparently those feelings wouldn't be denied. He *wanted* her to make demands of him, to push him into ending this ridiculous task so he could finally commit to her. But with each day that passed, it appeared as though Worthington was, indeed, guilty of treason and now Kerrick had no choice but to continue.

At least he'd finally received some news from the man he had following Worthington, news that indicated the Earl of Standish was somehow involved. He'd learned earlier that day that Worthington had met with Standish. The two had argued, but his man hadn't been able to get close enough to overhear them. He didn't understand why Standish would engage in treasonous activity any more than Worthington, but his instincts told him that their meeting was significant, and his instincts were rarely wrong.

That information had spurred him to sneak into Worthington's home earlier that evening after the family had left for tonight's ball. He'd searched Worthington's study thoroughly, hoping to find something, anything, that would allow him to put this entire matter behind him. He'd already informed Brantford about what he'd learned and warned him about his impending confrontation with Worthington. He'd also told him that he had no intention of actually becoming engaged to the Worthingtons' daughter. Brantford had taken it well, which strengthened Kerrick's suspicion that the man felt something for Rose Hardwick. Of course, Brantford would never act on that attraction.

He'd caught a glimpse of Catherine when he'd finally arrived, late, for the ball and had been avoiding her ever since. He'd spoken to Overlea and Louisa—to ignore them, as well, would rouse too many suspicions—but only when Catherine was dancing with someone else. He scanned the dancing couples and told himself he was looking for Rose.

There was a discreet cough to his left and he turned to find a young footman standing very close.

"My lord," he started, his voice low, "I've been told that your presence is requested in the library."

He raised a brow in surprise. "Who made the request?"

The young man shook his head. "I don't know. I received the instructions via a note from another member of the staff."

He closed his eyes briefly in exasperation, the vision of Worthington cornering him and making his demands clear in his mind. It looked like he would no longer be able to put off this confrontation.

But when he turned to follow the footman from the ballroom, he spied Worthington deep in conversation with someone else. He didn't even glance in Kerrick's direction, and with every step, Kerrick began to think that perhaps Catherine had sent the note. No one else would summon him in such a stealthy manner. Brantford certainly wouldn't—he'd approach him directly. But he hadn't seen Catherine in the past quarter hour at least.

Foolishly, anticipation began to sizzle through his veins. Meeting in such a public place was the height of insanity, especially given the fact that rumors about the two of them were already beginning to spread. But he couldn't dredge up any anger. This was what he'd wanted, after all. For Catherine to finally start making some demands of him.

He reached the open doorway where another footman nodded discreetly, indicating the direction he should go. He wondered briefly if the entire staff knew about this meeting and found he didn't care. He'd pointed Brantford in Standish's direction and couldn't wait to put the entire matter behind him. He hadn't found concrete proof of Worthington's guilt, but he'd learned enough to know the man definitely had secrets, and Kerrick knew in his bones that Standish was involved. As far as he was concerned, someone else could take over the investigation now and delve into Standish's dealings.

He'd half expected to find yet another footman outside the library, ready to open the door for him, but the hallway was empty. He slipped into the room, a smile already on his face. That smile turned into a frown when he found that the woman waiting for him was not Catherine, but Rose Hardwick. His disappointment appeared minor, however, when compared to the despair on Rose's face when she looked up and saw him. Her whole demeanor changed and she slumped into her chair with a mirthless laugh.

She lifted a hand to massage one of her temples. "Please don't tell me you're here to propose marriage."

He moved to take the seat opposite her and ignored

her statement. "It was you who wanted to see me."

"Please do not take offense," she said with a small shake of her head, "but you are the very last person I wished to see."

"Then why did you ask a footman to summon me?"

"I most certainly didn't." She straightened and removed one of her gloves. Inside the palm was a small folded note, which she handed to him. "I am here because I received that note, but I'd hoped it was someone else who'd sent it."

Kerrick unfolded the small piece of paper. On it was a single sentence asking Rose to wait in the library. It was unsigned. He glanced back at her. "I didn't send this. Further, I was told that someone wanted to meet me here."

"So we were both summoned. But why?"

"I have no idea, but I think it best we leave before someone discovers us alone together."

Rose nodded and when she stood, Kerrick rose as well.

"It was foolish of me to come, but I'd hoped…" She gave a small shake of her head. "Never mind what I had hoped. I do wonder, though. You couldn't hide your disappointment when you saw me. Where you hoping it was Catherine who wanted to see you?"

His whole ruse was crumbling down around him

and he no longer cared. "You are very direct."

Rose smiled. "She is my friend and she cares for you. Deeply. And I think you feel the same way about her. I don't want you to feel obliged to continue to court me because of some silly wish held by our mothers."

"You are also very perceptive."

"Good. So now we can put this entire episode behind us."

"It has been a pleasure, Miss Hardwick," he said, raising her hand to his mouth.

It was then that all hell broke loose. The door to the library was flung open, and he and Rose sprang apart, but not quickly enough. His stomach clenched when Lord and Lady Worthington burst into the room. Lady Worthington was clearly distressed at finding the two of them alone together, but her husband couldn't hide his satisfaction. To make matters worse, several other guests were gathered around the doorway. Kerrick felt his airway constricting as surely as if someone had placed a noose around his neck. A quick glance at Rose told him that she had come to the same realization that he had. Moments ago they'd agreed to part amicably, but now to save her reputation he had no choice but to announce their engagement and pray that his reckless behavior last night didn't mean Catherine was already carrying his child.

Kerrick spoke the words, much to the delight of the onlookers. One, in particular, looked on the scene with gleeful satisfaction. Standish.

He bowed, again, over Rose's hand, but this time he murmured some nonsense about how happy she had made him before excusing himself and heading for the door. He had just cleared the threshold when he froze. Headed toward him was Catherine, along with her sister and brother-in-law.

"We heard there was some kind of commotion," Louisa said when the group reached him. "What happened?"

"Lord Kerrick has just declared his intention to marry my daughter," Worthington said as he clapped him on the back. "Pay us a call tomorrow and we can start to make plans."

Kerrick ignored him. All he cared about in that moment was Catherine, and the look of utter devastation on her face before she turned and fled. Louisa followed, and it was only then that he turned to look at his best friend. The anger coming off Nicholas almost made him flinch, but he couldn't forget the expression on Standish's face and in that moment he knew. He'd originally thought that Worthington had planned this little encounter, but the man really wasn't that devious. It was Standish who'd arranged for him and Rose to be caught alone together, and he would only have done so for one reason. He wanted Catherine for himself. The thought chilled Kerrick to the bone.

He shook off Worthington's hand on his shoulder and approached Nicholas. "I believe Standish has designs on Catherine. Make sure he doesn't hurt her."

"More than you already have? I don't think that's possible."

The words, thrown out at him, were meant to hurt and they hit their mark. Kerrick said nothing more, knowing that he deserved the contempt clearly delineated in every muscle of Nicholas's body as the man turned his back and stalked away.

Standish approached Worthington then. It took an almost inhuman effort for Kerrick to resist the impulse to drag the smug bastard outside and beat him to a bloody pulp. Instead, with fists clenched at his sides to keep himself in check, he watched as the men exchanged a few words. Standish was turned away and Kerrick couldn't see his face, but he could see Worthington's. And what he saw there was a mixture of relief and fear.

So this was why Rose had told Catherine that her father seemed almost desperate for their union to be formally announced. Because Standish had demanded it. And like an idiot, he'd walked right into the trap.

He remained still when Standish approached him.

"I hear that congratulations are in order." The smug superiority on the man's face had Kerrick clenching his fists even tighter. Out of the corner of his eye, he didn't miss the fact that Worthington had turned to slink away, making sure to take his wife and daughter with him.

Most of the onlookers followed, but a few remained behind, no doubt waiting to see if there would be more to gossip about. But they were far enough away that they wouldn't overhear what Kerrick had to say.

"I know you orchestrated that."

Standish raised a brow. "Why would I do that?"

Standish was baiting him, but he didn't care. He had nothing left to lose, after all. "You mistake Overlea if you think he'll allow you anywhere near her."

The other man dropped his mask of civility. "I think you should concern yourself with your bride-to-be and leave Miss Evans to me," he said with a sneer. "Unlike you, I'm not afraid to take what I want."

Kerrick didn't stop to consider the repercussions of his actions. His fist slammed into Standish's face with a satisfying crunch. Standish stumbled back a few steps, disbelief and hatred etched on his face.

"I'll see you in hell first." Kerrick shook out his hand as he walked away, ignoring the whispers among those who had stayed behind to witness his confrontation with Standish.

His hand throbbed, but the pain didn't come close to touching the ache in his heart.

CHAPTER FIFTEEN

SHE IMAGINED THIS was what it would feel like to drown. First, the shock of cold when your body hit the water, followed by numbness as your extremities started to lose feeling, the struggle to keep the dark depths from swallowing you whole. The only thing that kept her afloat now was the certainty that Kerrick and Rose's engagement wasn't real. It couldn't be real, not after everything she and Kerrick had shared. Not after Rose had told her she wouldn't accept a proposal of marriage from him.

She'd been compromised... she had no choice but to accept.

Catherine ruthlessly squelched down the doubt that threatened her sanity. It wasn't real, she told herself over and over again as she waited for a note from Kerrick the next day. And when one didn't arrive, she remembered that she had told him she could no longer trust Lily to keep their notes a secret.

When Louisa suggested they stay home that evening, Catherine wouldn't hear of it. Her sister thought she was putting on a brave face and tried to insist, but it wasn't bravery that made her determined to attend yet another ball that evening. It was desperation. She was convinced that Kerrick would find a way to speak to her, to explain what was really happening.

When they entered the Abernathys' ballroom, it was impossible to miss the speculative glances cast her way, but she held her head high. She wasn't about to show any weakness in the face of the ever-hungry gossip mill.

While she feigned indifference on the surface, inside she was aware of everything going on around her. Kerrick had not yet arrived, and she did her best to keep from darting glances at the doorway every few minutes. She caught Rose looking her way and more than once thought her friend was going to approach her. But Rose's parents remained by her side, ever vigilant, and were quick to draw their daughter's attention away from her.

She allowed Thornton to dance with her twice. People were already gossiping about her, and she'd rather they turn their attention to speculation about future relationships than her heartbreak upon hearing of Kerrick and Rose's engagement. And when Thornton sought her out at various other times during the evening, at least his presence helped keep Lord Standish away. She'd been aware of the way he stared at her from the moment they'd arrived, and the almost-predatory expression on his face stretched her already frayed nerves even further.

She was aware of Kerrick's presence the moment he arrived. Even if she hadn't seen him making his way to where Rose was sitting on the other side of the ballroom, the pitying glances cast her way would have been impossible to miss. She told herself that she had to remain strong, and so she kept her smile firmly in place and accepted all invitations to dance. Even Lord Standish's. She couldn't help but recall how Kerrick had reacted the last time she'd danced with him, how he'd taken her aside and kissed her for the first time. She wasn't goading him intentionally, yet it was satisfying all the same when she caught his eye and saw his clear displeasure.

Unlike that other time, however, Louisa refused to

leave her side when she wasn't dancing. So when she headed for the ladies' retiring room, hoping that Kerrick would again waylay her on the way back, Louisa accompanied her.

But Kerrick did approach them upon their return to the ballroom. Despite the fact that he'd told her he would be careful not to be seen with her in public, she was certain he'd ask her to dance now. It was the only way he'd be able to speak to her in private. So she forced herself to accept his brief bow and waited, not so patiently, when he turned to speak to Louisa.

"I didn't dare approach you earlier," he said with a wry twist of his mouth. "I didn't want to give Nicholas the chance to call me out."

"You're not his favorite person right now, but I daresay he'll get over it."

Kerrick nodded in reply and then turned his attention to her. Only instead of asking her to dance, he just looked at her for several moments. As the silence stretched, she was finally struck by the reality of their situation. The misery reflected in his eyes could only mean one thing—his betrothal to Rose was genuine.

"I'm sorry... for everything," he managed before turning and walking away from them. From her.

Speechless, she could only stare at his back as he retreated. He couldn't have shocked her more if he had hit her.

She was barely aware of her sister linking her arm through hers and turning her away. "We'll leave shortly," she whispered and Catherine could only incline her head in reply.

A detached part of her mind recognized that she was in shock, and she welcomed the numbness. She'd feel later, but right now she had to keep from breaking down.

She didn't say anything when they reached her brother-in-law, who was chatting with the Claringtons. The sympathy in Charlotte's eyes told her that the duchess had witnessed their exchange with Kerrick, and it threatened to push Catherine over the edge. A quick glance at the men told her that they hadn't seen the interlude. Louisa had only to murmur something about feeling fatigued and Nicholas insisted on taking her home. But unlike that other evening when her sister and brother-in-law had left a house party early, no one said anything about Catherine spending the rest of the evening with the Claringtons acting as her chaperone.

Louisa kept up a steady stream of small talk as they made their way outside and waited for their carriage to be brought around. If Nicholas noticed her mood, he didn't say anything. The Overlea carriage was approaching when a flurry of activity captured their attention.

As one, they turned to see Lord Worthington exiting the Abernathy's home, flanked by two men. Everything about Worthington—his dead-eyed expression, the way his shoulders hunched in as though he were trying to make himself smaller—spoke of a man defeated. They watched as the small group moved to a carriage that was already waiting. Worthington didn't even glance their way as he climbed into the vehicle before being followed by the two men.

"I wonder what could have happened," Louisa said. "Worthington looks very upset."

"Not as upset as his wife and daughter."

At Nicholas's words, they turned back to see Rose and her mother exiting the house. Kerrick was only a step behind them, his expression grim. Lady Worthington appeared as though she were on the verge of collapse, and Kerrick moved to support her.

Catherine watched in silence as the small group moved down the street to where a group of carriages stood waiting. They didn't enter the same one as Lord Worthington, but continued past it to another.

Catherine was so immersed in her own misery that she couldn't find it within herself to wonder about the strange tableau they had just witnessed. The only thing she could focus on was the fact that Kerrick was already behaving as though he were part of the Worthington family.

"Catherine."

Her sister's voice dragged her away from her dark thoughts as she climbed into their carriage. Thankfully no one said a word during the drive home. She was convinced that was the only reason she was able to hold back her tears until she was safely back in her bedroom.

Was this love, then? The certainty that life would never again hold any joy if you couldn't spend it with the person who inspired that emotion?

It wasn't surprising that he loved Catherine Evans. On some level he supposed he'd known it all along. How could he not? And it wasn't just that she was beautiful, though she was that. It was everything else. She was kind, generous, but also incredibly maddening when she had made up her mind about something. She would never be content to remain in the background.

Her joy for the small things in life was delightful. The way her whole demeanor lit up when she was among her precious plants. The way she looked at him as though he could give her the very sun. And he found that he would be content to do that for her—spend his life trying to make her happy. And now he would never

251

have that opportunity. Even worse, if his recklessness when he visited her bedchamber bore fruit, he would be the cause of her ruin and would have to watch as she married someone else and raised their child with him.

If the melancholy he felt at that moment was love, he wanted none of it. He understood now why Nicholas had been so miserable the previous fall when he believed he could never have a future with Louisa. Why he'd drink himself into oblivion, knowing that alcohol would worsen the progress of the illness from which he had believed he was suffering. Kerrick had never been one to lose himself in the bottom of a bottle, but at that moment there was nothing he wanted more.

But he wouldn't. Worthington had confessed to committing treason, but it had come too late to save him from a loveless marriage. And such selfish wallowing wouldn't be fair to Rose, who wanted this marriage even less than he did. They were both trapped.

He hadn't been able to sleep, and so he gave up trying when the sun began to rise. He roamed the corridors of his house like a ghost, trying to will the hours to pass more quickly so he could go about setting things in motion. He and Rose would have to marry quickly if he hoped to shield her and her mother from the worst of the backlash that would come when word of Worthington's confession spread. To be honest, he wasn't sure how effective his protection would be, but he would do what he could. Rose and her mother would have to retire to the country and remain there for some time. Perhaps after a few years, as the scandal faded and new ones took its place, they'd be able to return to town again.

Brantford had likely stayed up as well, and he wondered idly if he'd questioned Worthington himself or had someone else do it. Regardless, he knew that Brantford would gather what information he could and then pay him a visit now that this mission was at an end.

That visit came just before noon.

"You look terrible," Brantford said after he'd been shown into the library.

Of course, Kerrick couldn't say the same for Brantford. He was, as always, impeccably groomed. He lounged casually in a chair and appeared as though he'd spent the night in long, restful slumber. Kerrick had no idea how the man always managed to look so detached from everything that was happening around him.

"What did you learn from Worthington?" he asked, ignoring Brantford's comment and sinking into a chair opposite him.

"Absolutely nothing beyond what we already know.

He's been selling secrets to the French about the movement of our navy. Information gleaned from his friendship with Admiral Nicholby. Of course, he was quick to point out that the Admiral wasn't involved and had no idea what he was doing."

"Do you believe him?"

Brantford raised a brow. "You don't?"

"I'm not sure," Kerrick said with a shake of his head. "This whole thing doesn't seem right. I'm sure he was passing on information and that Standish is somehow involved, but I can't figure out why. As much as I hate the bastard, he doesn't strike me as the type to betray his country for money. Not when he has more than both of us combined."

Brantford was silent for several moments, and Kerrick wondered if he was going to reveal anything more. He was, after all, now out of the whole business of ferreting out information for the Home Office.

"I think there's more to this than what we know so far," Brantford finally said. "We're trying to get more information from Worthington, but he refuses to name an accomplice. Says he was working alone."

"I suspect he's trying to protect his wife and daughter."

Brantford nodded, the motion almost absentminded, before asking, "What do you plan to do about Miss Hardwick?"

What, indeed. "I'm bound by my word and I won't go back on it. They'll need my protection now more than ever."

Brantford nodded again and was about to add something when the butler interrupted with a discreet rap on the doorframe.

"Excuse me, my lord, but there is a young woman here to see you."

His foolish heart leapt, thinking perhaps it was Catherine, but when the butler continued he learned that Rose was waiting in the drawing room with her maid. His heart sank. Of course it wasn't Catherine. She probably never wanted to see him again, a sentiment for which he couldn't fault her.

He turned to Brantford, but before the Earl could excuse himself, Rose swept past the butler and entered the room.

"Miss Hardwick," Kerrick said, rising from his chair. Brantford rose as well. "You shouldn't be here. I was planning to visit you and your mother this afternoon."

Rose laughed, the sound bitter. "Are you worried about my reputation? Well, it is far too late for such concern. My father's actions have already ruined me."

"We will weather this storm together," he said,

attempting to impart a confidence he was far from feeling.

"I should leave the two of you to speak," Brantford said.

But before he could do so, Rose turned to face him.

"You needn't worry that I will sully your reputation with my presence. What I have to say to Lord Kerrick will be brief, and there is no reason why you cannot hear it."

There was an edge to her tone, a hint of anger that surprised Kerrick. What surprised him more, however, was the hint of emotion on his friend's face. For a brief moment it almost appeared as though he wanted to comfort Rose, but then the telltale sign was gone almost before it had appeared, hidden behind Brantford's normal mask of indifference. But that fleeting emotion served to underscore Kerrick's suspicion that Brantford was not immune to Rose Hardwick's charms.

Rose's bravado was clearly an attempt on her part to hide her hurt. Thinking only to soothe her, he said, "I will call on you later this afternoon. Your mother should be included in our plans."

Rose tried to smile, but it turned out more a grimace. "That is precisely why I am here to speak to you. I wish to break our engagement."

Kerrick's heart gave a not-unexpected leap of joy, but he tamped down on the emotion. He couldn't leave Rose unprotected during this difficult time. Selfishly, he wanted nothing more than to embrace her offer before she changed her mind, but he wouldn't be able to live with himself if he did. Perversely, he also knew Catherine would never again respect him if he did. She was lost to him either way.

He closed the distance between them and took her hand between both of his and gave it a slight squeeze. "You are going through a difficult time right now and mustn't do anything you will come to regret."

"But you and Catherine—"

"Can never be," he said, cutting off that train of thought before she could continue.

The smile she gave him this time was genuine. "You are a good man, but you are not the man for me."

"Rose—"

"No." She pulled her hand from his and took a step back. "My mind is made up. I have already sent word to a few friends that I have broken our engagement. They shouldn't have heard about Father yet, so will have no reason to return my notes unopened."

"Don't do this," he said. "I can offer you protection, especially now when you and your mother most need it."

She shook her head, her chestnut curls dancing with the vigorous movement. "My father is not a traitor."

"He confessed," Brantford said.

Rose turned to face him. "He would never betray his country, and I mean to prove it. So you see"—she turned back to Kerrick—"there is no reason for your sacrifice. Father will be proven innocent and all will be as it should. Including you and Catherine."

He couldn't find the words to respond. Theirs would hardly be the first broken engagement the *ton* had seen, though it would be one of the shortest.

"I don't know what to say."

"Just tell me you'll make Catherine happy. She deserves it."

Brantford interrupted, picking up on that to which he'd been too distracted to pay attention. "If you have proof of your father's innocence, I can see that it reaches those who would be able to help him."

Rose's lips pressed briefly into a tight line before she answered him. "I thought you were anxious to depart. Are you certain you're not lowering yourself to address me directly?"

Kerrick's eyebrows rose at the bitter retort, but he remained silent.

"If you don't desire my assistance, Miss Hardwick, that is entirely up to you. I wish you luck in exonerating your father on your own."

They gazed at each other for several long moments before Rose replied. "We're not receiving callers—not that anyone will want to associate with us once it becomes known that my father has confessed to treason—but if you call tomorrow afternoon I'll make sure you're not turned away. Mama is most distressed, and I have already been away from her too long today."

Brantford nodded in reply, and without another word Rose turned and departed.

"I'm out of it," Kerrick said before Brantford could speak.

"Of course," the other man said. "You can hardly be seen skulking about Worthington's home now that everyone will be learning of your broken engagement. Unless, of course, you hope to make her change her mind."

"I think you already know my opinion on that course of action. Rose Hardwick is all yours."

Brantford raised a brow in answer and Kerrick laughed. Suddenly the world seemed brighter, and he couldn't resist needling his friend about the beautiful young woman who didn't appear to be intimidated by the Unaffected Earl. "What was it you said when you first approached me about this matter? It would hardly be a hardship to court her."

"Marriage is not for me, my friend. Not now and perhaps not ever." Brantford's face was a blank mask, but Kerrick could now detect a hint of something behind it. Loneliness?

"Never say never, old chap."

CHAPTER SIXTEEN

SHE WAS DYING inside, but Catherine was determined to go through the motions of living. After seeing Rose and Kerrick together, she allowed herself one day locked away in her bedroom, wallowing in her misery and railing against the fates.

When the sun rose on the second day, instead of pulling the blankets over her head and burrowing deeper under them, which was what she wanted most to do, she cast them aside and rose. A quick glance at the mirror on her dressing table revealed signs she'd cried herself to sleep the previous night etched clearly on her face. Swollen eyelids, a nose that was still slightly red, and a complexion that was heightened with a pink tinge.

Turning her back on the reflection, she moved to the washstand, poured cold water from the pitcher into the bowl, and splashed her face, hoping to wash away the cursed proof of her heartache. The cold water wasn't a miracle cure, but it would help. Only time would take care of the rest of the outward signs. The inward signs would linger for some time, but she refused to give in to indulging that misery. If she'd learned one thing growing up in a family that could afford nothing beyond the bare necessities, it was that life always marched onward. Nothing was ever gained by allowing oneself to dwell on the impossible.

She wished she could say she didn't have regrets about her relationship with Kerrick, but the truth was that she did. She wished now that she had never acted so impetuously and gone to his town house that first time they'd made love. She would still have been heartbroken, but she couldn't help but think the pain she'd have experienced would be nothing to the soul-deep despair threatening to crush her now.

And the worst of it was that she couldn't be angry with Kerrick. He'd had no plans to begin a relationship with her while he was engaged in the inquiry that forced him into pretending to court Rose Hardwick. It had been her own foolishness that had led her to pursue an intimate relationship with him. Catherine could understand now why Louisa had wanted her to be careful in her dealings with him. Her sister clearly knew that life did not always hand out happy endings. The fact that she and Nicholas had achieved that seemingly impossible state did not blind Louisa to the pitfalls that lay out in the world, ready to ensnare young fools like herself.

The fact that Kerrick had offered to marry Rose after they were discovered alone together, despite the fact that he did not feel any romantic attachment to her, spoke volumes about his nature. And it was one of the main reasons she loved him still. She'd had her doubts about his feelings for Louisa, but now, with a clarity that could only be gained by hindsight, she knew that he hadn't seen her as merely a substitute for her sister.

Doing her best to shake off her melancholy thoughts, Catherine rang for her maid. She could tell that Lily was surprised to see her up and out of bed. The awareness that the servants knew what had happened, that they'd been gossiping about her belowstairs, made her cringe. It had been less than a year since Louisa had married and they'd moved to Overlea Manor, and she still wasn't used to having servants. It was more difficult than she would have imagined to know that all their lives were no doubt being examined and dissected by others.

She wouldn't give them anything more to gossip about and proceeded to dress as though it were any other morning, then headed downstairs.

Breakfast, however, proved to be more awkward than she'd anticipated. She had grown used to having breakfast alone in her room, but Louisa and Nicholas must have decided to join her when they learned she hadn't asked for her customary breakfast tray in her room.

Louisa took very small bites from a piece of toast, the effort appearing to cost her a great deal. Catherine expected it was sheer force of will alone that kept her sister from jumping up from the table and emptying the contents of her stomach. She and Nicholas alternated between watching her carefully and turning their attention back to their plates.

Catherine ate quickly, anxious to be away from the tense environment. She'd just finished her tea when Nicholas slammed his fork down on the table. She jumped in surprise but didn't miss the look that Louisa aimed at her husband.

"I can't remain silent," he told his wife before turning to face Catherine. "Kerrick is like a brother to me, but if he has laid even a finger on you, I will call him out."

"No, you won't," Louisa said.

His expression was one of incredulous disbelief. "How can you say that? We all knew he was courting Rose Hardwick, yet he did nothing to dissuade Catherine from pinning her hopes on him."

"You know what he does. There may have been reasons—"

"His reasons can go to the devil, and him right along with them."

Catherine felt her carefully constructed façade begin to crack. She couldn't do this right now. Her hold on her sanity was tenuous at best. She stood and both of them turned their attention back to her. They'd been so focused on their own argument it was almost as though they'd forgotten she was even in the room.

"Nothing happened between us. Nothing that wasn't of my own imagination."

Nicholas scowled. "Don't feel that you have to lie to protect him."

She wanted to say more but couldn't. Emotion clogged her throat and she knew that one more syllable from her, or one more look of sympathy from her sister, would see her dissolving in a puddle of tears. Before that could happen, she turned and fled from the room, only to be brought up short by the flurry of activity in the front hall.

Louisa had followed her from the breakfast room and stopped beside her, waiting while the butler spoke to the two burly men in the doorway.

"My lady," he said to Louisa when he noticed the two of them standing there. He glanced past them and Catherine knew that Nicholas had joined them. "My lord, I was just informing these gentlemen that deliveries are to be made at the kitchen door.

The men seemed to take umbrage at his statement. "We're not deliverymen," one of them said, stepping farther into the hallway. The butler tried to stop him, but he was no match for the stout fellow. "We work for Kew Gardens and are here as a favor to the Earl of Kerrick."

Just the mention of his name caused a quick stab of pain to go through her. Louisa turned to her for clarification, but Catherine could only shake her head in bewilderment. "I don't know what it could be. He said nothing to me."

Louisa turned to her husband. "Nicholas?"

His jaw tightened and his hands had clenched into fists. "He certainly wouldn't be sending me anything from Kew Gardens."

Catherine closed her eyes, a horrible presentiment settling over her. They'd never spoken of it, but somehow she knew what the men were there to deliver.

"The tree is potted and we can bring it 'round to the back of the house if you have a garden. But there are very specific instructions for its care. I can't just leave it here until I know it will be properly looked after. It is quite valuable…"

Catherine wasn't aware she'd started moving until she'd pushed past the two startled men and stepped out onto the front steps of the town house. There, on the back of a large wagon drawn by two horses, stood a moderately sized orange tree.

Memories she'd been trying so hard to keep at bay swept over her then. She could still recall every detail of that first outing at Kew Gardens with the Duke and Duchess of Clarington when Kerrick had first arrived in London. How he'd arranged to have the head gardener himself escort them for most of their tour. And, of course, there had been their trip to the orangery. It was there that something had changed between them, and Kerrick had finally started to see her as a woman and not just Louisa's younger sister. She'd thought him bored beyond reason during most of their visit, yet he'd been patient. And clearly he'd taken note of her interest in the orange trees.

She wouldn't be able to keep it once summer ended. Mr. Clifton had explained how the trees were not receiving enough light at the orangery and were suffering during the winter months, and she didn't think they'd fare any better at the conservatory attached to Overlea Manor. It seemed that, like Kerrick himself, she wouldn't be able to keep this gift.

Somehow she turned and faced the group of people who were watching her in silence and managed to keep her voice even when she spoke. "I met with Mr. Clifton and remember what he told me about their care."

She wanted to say more but found she could no longer hold back the crush of emotions threatening to engulf her. She didn't need to ask to be excused. The group split in two and in silence she took the path they'd opened up. She heard Louisa speaking to the men, telling them to bring the orange tree to the back garden through the mews, but her destination was the music room toward the rear of the house. If she returned to her bedroom now, she wouldn't be able to hold back her tears.

She'd almost made it when a voice stopped her cold.

"I don't care what you plan to do to me, but I must speak to Catherine."

Kerrick.

She heard footsteps. Fear gripped her as she stood frozen to the spot, unsure whether she should flee the remaining few steps to the music room or turn around.

Somehow she knew he wouldn't be deterred by her brother-in-law who, despite his assertions to the contrary, would never harm one of his closest friends.

The footsteps stopped and a short silence followed before he finally spoke. "Catherine."

Gathering her courage, she turned to face him. When she did, she realized she'd been hoping to see some indication that he felt even a fraction of the anguish she didn't think would ever leave her. But instead he seemed remarkably calm. In fact, he didn't appear sad at all. For the first time since all her hopes had been dashed, the stirrings of anger ignited within.

"I believe we've already said all there is to say. If you came to apologize, you needn't have wasted your time." She darted a quick look at Louisa and Nicholas, aware that they were listening to every word she spoke with keen interest. While she was hurt, and the temptation to lash out at him in anger was growing with swiftness, she'd promised Kerrick she wouldn't reveal just how far their relationship had developed. It was a promise she meant to keep and so she chose her next words with care. "I understand that you had little choice in how things played out. Now, if you'll excuse me."

She started this time for the stairway. The music room wasn't far enough away from everyone and the tears pricking the back of her eyes wouldn't be denied for much longer.

"Catherine, please. I must speak to you."

She heard him begin to follow and fought against the almost overwhelming urge to run.

"Let go of me, Nicholas, or you'll lose your hand," she heard him say.

"Haven't you already hurt her enough?"

"I'm not leaving until we've spoken," he called after her. "I'll haunt your doorway if I have to. Eventually you will speak to me."

She halted and brushed angrily at a tear that had escaped. She couldn't speak to him and keep a hold of the tenuous grip she currently had on her dignity. But it appeared there would be no way out of the impending confrontation. She closed her eyes for a moment, took a deep, shaky breath, and turned to face him.

"I was headed to the music room. We can speak there."

She didn't wait to see if he would be allowed to follow. The voices of her family warred with Kerrick's. Nicholas didn't want to allow it, but Louisa urged him to allow them five minutes together. Catherine had just crossed the threshold into the music room when she heard her brother-in-law reluctantly agree.

She walked over to the windows, which overlooked

their small back garden. The gardeners were just bringing in the orange tree, the two of them straining under the weight of the large pot holding it.

Dread settled in the pit of her stomach. The very last thing she wanted was to face Kerrick right now—her emotions were still too raw. She continued to watch the gardeners in silence as Kerrick entered the room and moved to stand beside her.

"I'm so sorry—"

"The orange tree was extravagant. You shouldn't have gone to the trouble or the expense."

"I have five minutes before Nicholas comes in here and beats me to a bloody pulp. I don't intend to waste that time making small talk."

She gave her head a small shake. "I can't…" She had to take a deep breath before she could find the strength to turn and face him. "You should go. There's nothing more to be said. Any fantasies I might have had about a future with you are now a thing of the past. And the very last thing I need to hear right now is your apology."

She started for the door, but he reached out and gripped her arm, halting her progress. She tried to pull away but was no match for his strength. He pulled her toward him and grasped her other hand.

It hurt too much to look at him and so she gazed,

instead, at their joined hands.

"I'm not marrying Rose."

Her head snapped up at that softly spoken statement, and for a moment she feared her grief was causing her to lose track of her faculties. But the way his mouth lifted at the corners, the slight gleam in his eyes that hinted at anything but sorrow, led her to believe otherwise. She couldn't keep the slight tremble from her voice as she asked, "What did you say?"

He lifted her hands to his mouth and dropped kisses on her fingers before replying. "I'm not marrying Rose. She's already started to spread word that she's broken our engagement."

Emotions warred within her, but the one that stood at the forefront was joy. Kerrick wasn't going to marry another woman… one whom she'd come to think of as a good friend. "You won't be marrying Rose." She repeated the words with wonder, allowing herself to actually believe they were true.

His smile broadened. "No. But that leads me to another subject. Since I'm in danger of being dragged out of here at any moment, I don't have the luxury of time. I probably don't deserve such happiness—not after the hurt I caused you—but I'm selfish enough to cling to the hope that you'll consent to be my wife."

Words escaped her. That he could even doubt she'd

say yes... She could only nod, tears of happiness threatening to overwhelm her as he dragged her into his arms.

"Thank God," he said, his arms tightening around her. "I was afraid you'd never forgive me. I'm not sure I would have were I in your shoes."

She shook her head and looked up at him in wonder. "There could never be anyone else for me. That you could doubt me—"

"No, never that. I feared, though, that you would doubt the depth of my love for you. After what I put you through..." He closed his eyes for a brief moment, and she could see the self-recrimination etched on his face. "I can't even begin to express how angry I am with myself for causing you such hurt. I never should have allowed myself to indulge my desire for you. Not until after my assignment was over."

She caressed his cheek, unable to believe that he would take all the blame for their relationship onto himself. "I didn't give you a choice."

He laughed at that. "No, you didn't. But to be honest, I'm not sure I would have been able to stop myself even without your encouragement. Still, despite the fact that I knew you cared for me, you had me worried." He stopped and she could sense him warring with whether to continue.

"Why?"

"Thornton and all those others vying for your attention… I kept expecting you to decide I wasn't worth the bother."

"You would not be the man I loved if you had stood back and allowed Rose's reputation to fall into ruin. While a part of me hated you for that, another part loved you all the more."

He closed his eyes for a brief moment and the remaining tension in his body drained away.

"So it was Rose who broke the engagement?"

He nodded in reply. "In the end, she was the noblest of us all."

Catherine shook her head. "She cares for another. She is a dear friend, but her willingness to suffer the gossip following a broken engagement was not just for the two of us. She never told me who it was she cares for, but I can only hope that whoever he is, he is worthy of her."

His expression turned grave. "I'm not sure anyone would have her now."

She sucked in her breath and let it out in a rush. "Her father…"

He nodded. "Worthington confessed to passing confidential information to the French."

"So he was guilty after all. Poor Rose," she said, a

pang of regret for her friend going through her. "We must do everything we can for her. I will not abandon her."

"I wouldn't expect you to. I also happen to agree, especially since I'm not at all certain his involvement in the whole scheme was voluntary."

Catherine pulled back at that. "So we can still help her? What can I do?"

"No," Kerrick said, drawing her back into his arms. "I am out of it, as are you. You'll have to settle for living the life of an ordinary countess."

"But we must help Rose—"

"She has the best help available to her at the moment. And no," he said, placing a finger over her lips to still the questions that sprang to mind, "I won't tell you who that is."

She drew his finger into her mouth and his gaze zeroed in on her lips, his eyes darkening. "I think I can guess," she said after releasing him. "He has fair hair and also happens to be an earl—"

His mouth settled over hers and she leaned into him, taking comfort from the knowledge that there would now be many more kisses in her future. She made a soft sound of protest when he drew back.

He shook his head slightly as if to clear it. "Nicholas won't stop to hear our news if he finds us in a passionate embrace." He looked toward the door, a slight frown on his brow as she took a step back. "I'm surprised he hasn't already barged in here."

Catherine already missed Kerrick's touch. "Louisa probably distracted him. She's very good at that."

A fond smile crossed his face. "The Evans sisters appear to have that in common."

His obvious affection for her sister reminded her of how close the two had seemed when he'd stayed at Overlea Manor. She took a deep breath and asked the final question she needed answered. "You'll tell me what happened between the two of you last year?" She hesitated before continuing. "At times I feared you and Louisa were more than friends."

"No, never that," he said, taking her hand and squeezing it in reassurance. "I know it appeared that way and I'll tell you everything when we have more time. I think we're going to need to share our news, though. Your sister won't be able to hold Nicholas back for very long. He's very protective of you."

Catherine nodded, but her eyes were drawn to the window and the extravagant, yet impractical, gift he had sent. He must have seen her disappointment.

"You don't like the orange tree?"

"It's lovely and so rare in England. I can't believe you managed to get Mr. Clifton to part with it."

"It wasn't faring well there. I assured him that you would be able to nurse it back to health."

It was clear he didn't realize she wouldn't be able to do that. "The light isn't any stronger at Overlea Manor. The conservatory has the same large windows as those at the orangery. If we keep it there, the tree will eventually go into decline. We will have to find another home for it."

"I never intended for the tree to go to your sister and brother-in-law."

There was a gleam in his eye and her heart rate sped up. "But your estate—"

"Doesn't have a conservatory, no. But I have made arrangements for an architect to visit within the week. I plan to put in a proper greenhouse. Of course, my future wife will have the last say about its design."

She squealed and threw herself into his arms, no longer caring that her sister and brother-in-law might walk in at any moment. Kerrick clearly felt the same way because when she lifted her face, eager for his kiss, he accepted her invitation. And this time he didn't hold back from showing her just how much he'd missed her.

THE END

Rose and Brantford's story continues in *The Unaffected Earl*, book 3 in the Landing a Lord series. To learn when the book is available, please take a moment to sign up for Suzanna's mailing list at http://eepurl.com/nmliD.

AUTHOR'S NOTE

THANK YOU FOR reading *Beguiling the Earl*. If you enjoyed reading this book, please consider sharing it with a friend. All honest reviews are welcome and appreciated.

The head gardener at Kew Gardens at the time this story takes place was William Townsend Aiton. I wasn't sure how much of a day-to-day role he had at Kew Gardens—he was also in charge of the gardens at Kensington and Buckingham Palaces—so I decided to invent the character of George Clifton to act in the role of head gardener.

The history of Kew Royal Botanic Gardens is very rich, and I could only touch on it briefly. When one considers that history, it is not hard to understand why Catherine Evans was so eager to visit. Kew Gardens had already gained international recognition during the 1800s because of its large collection of exotic plants.

That was due in large part to botanist Sir Joseph Banks (1743-1820), who was President of the Royal Society for over forty-one years. He made various overseas plant-hunting expeditions himself and financed other voyages. In fact, during the early 1800s, all ships that returned from British colonies brought with them plant specimens for Kew Gardens.

Also, yes, I included another waltz in this book even though such an intimate dance was not common in London in 1807. I hope you'll forgive the creative liberty I took in including it here.

If you'd like to learn more about my books, please visit my website at:

http://www.suzannamedeiros.com

or visit me on Facebook at:

http://www.facebook.com/AuthorSuzannaMedeiros

To learn when I have a new release available, you can sign up for my mailing list at http://eepurl.com/nmliD. I promise never to spam or to share your email address.

Thank you again for reading Catherine and Kerrick's story. I hope you enjoyed their journey and I hope you join me for the next book!

Suzanna

The Unaffected Earl—book 3 in the Landing a Lord series—will be available in 2015.

They call him the Unaffected Earl…
Many seek his favor, men and women alike, but few glimpse what lies beneath the Earl of Brantford's aloof exterior.

She was the woman everyone wanted…
Rose Hardwick was the most sought after debutante in London until scandal touched her family and made her a social pariah.

He alone has the power to help her…
Rose is determined to prove her father innocent of the crime of treason, but first she must convince the Unaffected Earl to help her. When circumstances force them closer together, will she be able to thaw the ice that encases his heart?

ABOUT THE AUTHOR

Suzanna Medeiros was born and raised in Toronto, Canada. Her love for the written word led her to pursue a degree in English Literature from the University of Toronto. She went on to earn a Bachelor of Education degree, but graduated at a time when no teaching jobs were available. After working at a number of interesting places, including a federal inquiry, a youth probation office, and the Office of the Fire Marshal of Ontario, she decided to pursue her first love—writing.

Suzanna is married to her own hero and is the proud mother of twin daughters. She is an avowed romantic who enjoys spending her days writing love stories.

She would like to thank her parents for showing her that love at first sight and happily ever after really do exist.

SUZANNA MEDEIROS

BEGUILING THE EARL

SUZANNA MEDEIROS

34048555R00177

Made in the USA
Middletown, DE
22 January 2019